CLARITY

QUEER SCI FI'S NINTH ANNUAL FLASH FICTION CONTEST

Published by
Other Worlds Ink
PO Box 19341, Sacramento, CA 95819

Cover art © 2022 by J. Scott Coatsworth. Cover content is for illustrative purposes only and any person depicted on the cover is a model.

Clarity © 2022 by Queer Sci Fi

All rights reserved. This book is licensed to the original purchaser only. Duplication or distribution by any means is illegal and a violation of international copyright law, subject to criminal prosecution and upon conviction, fines, and/or imprisonment. Any eBook format cannot be legally loaned or given to others. No part of this book can be reproduced or transmitted in any form or by any means, electronic or mechanical, including photocopying, recording, or by any information storage and retrieval system, without the written permission of the Publisher, except where permitted by law.

To request permission and all other inquiries, contact Other Worlds Ink, PO Box 19341, Sacramento, CA 95819, or https://www.otherworldsink.com.

❦ Created with Vellum

CONTENTS

Foreword ... ix

FANTASY PART ONE

Telegram From the Netherland ... 3
Alex Liddell (255 words)

Ascension ... 5
W. Dale Jordan (298 words)

Looped ... 7
K.S. Murphy (297 words)

Age Cannot Wither Her ... 9
Barbara Krasnoff (299 words)

Upon Reflection ... 10
Shirley Meier (298 words)

Ghosts ... 11
Warren Rochelle (297 words)

Impulse ... 13
Jaime Munn (300 words)

Refraction ... 15
Gordon Bonnet (293 words)

Lovers' Letters ... 17
Ginger Streusel (298 words)

Ruti's Prayer ... 19
Lloyd A. Meeker (297 words)

Orange Dust ... 21
Nicole Dennis (300 words)

Willows ... 23
Amanda Meuwissen (300 words)

If the Shoe Fits ... 24
SI CLARKE (299 words)

Arene, 27F, Invisible ... 26
A. B. Encarnacion (299 words)

SCIENCE FICTION PART ONE

Post-Apocalyptic Goo ... 31
Devon Widmer (300 words)

Bathtub Gin ... 33
Andrea Stanet (299 words)

Impact ... 35
Sage HN (298 words)

Oysters and Other Slimy Creatures 37
Allan Dyen-Shapiro (300 words)

Cycles 39
Scott Jenson (296 words)

The Best Solution 41
David Viner (297 words)

The Shadow of Doubt 43
Nathan Alling Long (300 words)

Blue 45
Kayleigh Sky (299 words)

Meet Me at the South Gate 47
Alma Nilssom (299 words)

Sad Reality 49
Stephen B. Pearl (298 words)

Harmony 50
Jaymie Wagner (298 words)

The Truth Sayer 52
Caro Soles (292 words)

Cold Conviction 53
Jennifer Haskin (291 words)

Heartsbeats 54
Jendayi Brooks-Flemister (291 words)

PARANORMAL

A Grey Man 57
Terry Poole (297 words)

The Glimpse 59
Anne Smith (292 words)

The Ghost Maid 60
Crysta K. Coburn (298 words)

Never Alone 62
Rin Sparrow (300 words)

Verity 64
Julie Bozza (278 words)

Shinigami 65
A. J. Clarke (296 words)

The Vampire and the Werewolf Priest 67
Darrell Z. Grizzle (299 words)

If Deliberate Avoidance Fulfills No Dream 69
Yoyoli (299 words)

Beneath the Surface 71
Kaje Harper (300 words)

Alice! 73
Rdp (293 words)

The Man in the Mirror 74
Steve Rasnic Tem (300 words)

Fresh *A.H. Lykke (291 words)*	76
The World Around Her *Joe DeRouen (299 words)*	77

FANTASY PART TWO

Franklin *Jordan Ulibarri (300 words)*	81
Clearing the Heir *Gina Storm Grant (283 words)*	83
Death by Siren *Alex Blanc (300 words)*	85
Outpouring *Catherine Yeates (294 words)*	86
A Smoking Hot Proposal *Sheryl R. Hayes (297 words)*	88
The Chase Was Enough *C.T. Phipps (280 words)*	90
Sea-Glass *Isobel Granby (300 words)*	91
With Clear Eyes *Mere Rain (249 words)*	92
The Face in the Mirror *RoAnna Sylver (297 words)*	94
Bloom *JS Gariety (300 words)*	96
Crystal Clear *Rainie Zenith (298 words)*	98
No Crime Unseen *Blaine D. Arden (294 words)*	100
The Unicorn's Knight *K.L. Noone (299 words)*	102

SCIENCE FICTION PART TWO

Through This Window *Monique Cuillerier (298 words)*	107
Brain of Theseus *James Dunham (300 words)*	109
The Art of Not Blowing Up *Isabel McKeough (300 words)*	111
Shared Language *Kim Fielding (291 words)*	113
Clouds *Alden Loveshade (296 words)*	115

Bowls of Steaming Noodles — 117
Jane Suen (299 words)

The Furthest Horizon — 119
Isa Reneman (296 words)

Wrinkled — 121
Raven Oak (292 words)

Crystal Clear — 122
D.M. Rasch (298 words)

Male Female Nonbinary Other — 124
RE Andeen (299 words)

Overcoming Entropy — 126
William R. Eakin (298 words)

Software Update — 127
Derwin Mak (289 words)

Hindsight — 129
J Sigel (298 words)

FANTASY PART THREE

My Poppy Fields Are Burning — 133
Krystle Matar (300 words)

Stagecoach Mary Versus the Ghost of Cascade — 135
Jess Nevins (299 words)

Muddy the Waters — 137
M. X. Kelly (300 words)

Demons Need Love Too — 139
Stacy Noe (299 words)

Magically Induced Clarity — 141
Izzy Tyack (200 words)

Translucent — 143
Steve Fuson (300 words)

The Choice — 145
Belinda McBride (295 words)

The Cursed Princess — 147
Jamie Lackey (298 words)

The Satyr and the Wishing Pond — 149
Kiya Nicoll (297 words)

The Gift — 151
Megan Hippler (298 words)

Visus — 153
Kris Jacen (296 words)

Remote Working Gothic — 155
Jamie Sands (302 words)

SCIENCE FICTION PART THREE

Make Me Real *Daria Richter (290 words)*	159
Smile *Alex Silver (296 words)*	161
Stuck in the Space Elevator *A Acosta (300 words)*	163
Through a Glass Clearly *Stephen Dedman (297 words)*	165
The Only Question I Could Ask *Drew Baker (268 words)*	167
Detonation *Anton Kukal (300 words)*	168
The Blue Capsule Experience *Josie Kirkwood (297 words)*	170
Sunrise *Kora Knight (300 words)*	172
Earth Day *E. W. Murks (300 words)*	174
A Visage of Home *Tori Thompson (300 words)*	176
Burden of the Blurred *Camryn Burke (298 words)*	178
Unexpected	180
New Memories *T.J. Reed (300 words)*	182
A Trick of the Nerves *RL Mosswood (299 words)*	184

HORROR

Inflection Point *Elizabeth Hawxhurst (237 words)*	187
The Closet is Made of Mahogany *Megan Diedericks (300 words)*	188
Sunset *Emmy Eui (299 words)*	190
The Killer Cupid *Phoebe Ching (300 words)*	191
Blood Will Show Us Who We Are *V. Astor Solmon (297 words)*	193
Ribbon Thread *Megan Baffoe (290 words)*	194
PSI Ecstasy *Rob Bliss (291 words)*	196

The Sitter *R.L.Merrill (297 words)*	197
There's Something Weird About Joe *Patricia Loofbourrow (298 words)*	199
Kids Know *Abbie Bernstein (300 words)*	201
Happy to Help *Alison J. McKenzie (295 words)*	203
Matthias *Chloe Schaefer (300 words)*	205
A Woman's Reward *R.E. Carr (300 words)*	207
ACAB *Jason Sárközi-Forfinski (300 words)*	209

FANTASY PART FOUR

Magic Mirror *Lori Alden Holuta (300 words)*	213
Secundum Artem *Minerva Cerridwen (249 words)*	215
Through the Glass *Antonia Aquilante (299 words)*	216
The Night Witch *Rie Sheridan Rose (294 words)*	218
Murcorpio *Oskar Leonard (299 words)*	219
One Night in Troy *Rory Ni Coileain (300 words)*	221
The Unicorn Handler *Beáta Fülöp (298 words)*	223
The Gauntlet *Nathaniel Taff (297 words)*	225
Blood and Water *Siri Paulson (299 words)*	227
Taking the Plunge *Avery Vanderlyle (297 words)*	228
As Foretold *Marie Robertson (299 words)*	230
Late Bloomer *Mary Kuna (300 words)*	232
The Star Beast *Sacchi Green (298 words)*	234
About Queer Sci Fi & Other Worlds Ink	236

FOREWORD

It's hard to tell a story in just 300 words, so it's only fair that I limit this foreword to exactly 300 words, too. This year, 312 writers took the challenge, with stories across the queer spectrum. The contest rules are simple. Submit a complete, well-written Clarity-themed 300 word sci-fi, fantasy, paranormal or horror story with LGBTQ+ characters.

For our ninth year and eighth anthology, we chose the theme "Clarity." The interpretations run from an "Aha!" moment to the bubbling laughter of water to a private, life-changing realization. There are little jokes, big surprises, and future prognostications that will make your head spin.

I'm proud that this collection includes many colors of the LGBTQ+ (or QUILTBAG, if you prefer) universe—lesbian, gay, bisexual, transgender, intersex, queer, and asexual characters populate these pages—our most diverse contest yet. There's a bit of romance, too—and a number of stories solidly on the "mainstream" side. Flash fiction is short, fun, and easy to read. You may not fall in love with every story—in fact, you probably won't. But if you don't like one, just move on to the next, and you're sure to find some bite-sized morsels of flash fiction goodness. There are so many good stories in here—choose your own favorites.

We chose three winning stories, five judges' choice picks, and one director's pick, all marked in the text. Thanks to our judges—Angel Martinez, B.A. Brock, Ava Kelly, Lexi Ander, and J.M. Dabney—for selflessly giving their time, love, and energy to this project. And to Ryane Chatman too, for editing.

At Queer Sci Fi, we're building a community of writers and readers who want a little rainbow in their speculative fiction. Join us and submit a story of your own next time!

FANTASY PART ONE

Russell stared at his hands. His fingers were translucent to the first joint. Ghost disease, stage 1. He hid them with skingloves, terrified someone would see, turn him in, and he'd wind up in the quarantine barracks, and never be seen again.

— WARREN ROCHELLE, *GHOSTS*

TELEGRAM FROM THE NETHERLAND
ALEX LIDDELL (255 WORDS)

JUDGE'S CHOICE – Lexi Ander

For the attention of Archibald Terrabane,
  Sent by Veritas Yorrage.
  My stars Archie you will not believe what has happened at the precipice!
  I am aghast, agog, and frustrated beyond man's capacity for understanding.
  That page you sent me, the one with the hat and the badge with the pronouns? Ze has the eternal crystal. I'm devastated, flabbergasted and I needed to tell you before the official scribes relay it to the university, it's an embarrassment.
  Ze was barely here a day, two days later than you promised may I add, and I was recounting the translation on the walls which took me the better part of a year to decipher with the gracious help of the local mages.
  No sooner did I finish pondering the sentence "no man nor woman shall cross this ledge", ze, would you believe it, began crossing the ledge. Crossing the ledge with full unearned confidence no less, much to the horror of everyone at the expedition camp. We screamed at zir to halt because, as I previously thought I made clear, nobody had survived the journey across the ledge.
  Poor Camilla was inconsolable. I was inconsolable. We're still shaken truth be told.
  It was grossly irresponsible and a needless risk on zir part. To all our surprise however, ze somehow miraculously returned, crystal in hand with no word of apology. None.

The only thing ze said in zir defence was "that clears a few things up at least". Now tell me Archie, what in the world does that mean?!

I'm a bit of a gamer at heart and I love fantasy movies. I really adore the ones where there is a prophecy like, "No Man Can..." and then someone comes along and does it. Makes me so happy. Telegram from the Netherland runs along the lines of both themes and I loved it at first read. This is a letter from what I'd call the field archeologist, Veritas Yorrage, to their supporting university, Archibald Terrabane. The communication is smothered in narcissism and what should be momentous news is instead a letter of chastisement. The page sent by Archie was not only late, but does the unthinkable and everyone is traumatized and inconsolable. I laughed my butt off and applauded the page for knowing zirself and doing what 'no man or woman' could do. LOVED IT.

—Lexi Ander

ASCENSION
W. DALE JORDAN (298 WORDS)

I am invisible.

Unseen.

Unknown.

I know this because of the way people bump into me on the street. They are grey, grey, grey. Faceless, featureless. Stale, living zombies going about their lives, working their jobs, raising their children.

Drab, lifeless hetero-patriarchy swallowed the world centuries ago, and I am its unseen prisoner.

I sit on the sidewalk, watching their shambling footsteps, listening to their colorless conversations. They terrify me, and yet there are days I would give up my light, my color, to be seen. Just once.

"It's not that they can't see you," a voice says behind me, and I turn far too quickly, shading my eyes from the colors that assault them. "They *choose* not to see you. You are stardust surrounded by sullen, envious ash."

He shimmers.

"So do you."

Did he read my mind?

"I don't have to."

"I—"

"Focus," he says, and I do.

Slowly, almost impossibly, I see through his prismatic light. His features sharpen. His eyes are green. His hair is black. His skin is like ivory. His linen clothing is pale blue. He is clear, free, and unabashedly himself.

"Ira," he says, extending his hand to me.

His skin is warm, welcoming. I feel it spread throughout my body.

"Jonathan," I reply, smiling.

He flashes a beautiful smile before lifting my hand to kiss it.

"I see you," he says.

"Where are you from?" I ask, and he looks toward the sky then back to me.

"Do you want to be free?"

"Yes," I gasp before the question is fully formed, knowing I can never live in the dreary greyness again.

His movements are graceful, and the arms he wraps around me are strong. I lay my head against his chest as our feet leave the earth behind.

LOOPED
K.S. MURPHY (297 WORDS)

Avalon woke again with a horrified gasp, bolting upright and grabbing their throat. Soaked in sweat, they tried to rub the pain away as a few tears dripped from their chin. Familiar footsteps, echoing off stone walls, already came closer.

"It's time, Mx. Brookes."

Eyes flicking up, Avalon fought back another round of tears. Their heart twisted seeing him on the other side of these bars.

"Hello, Brighton."

A twitch of a smile. "Most people call me Pastor."

"I'm not most people."

"Oh?"

"I'm your spouse, Brighton."

"People on death row," he replied with sympathy, "often become confused on the day of their execution."

Avalon smothered a sob.

"Please," they whispered. "Don't let them kill me again."

"Mx. Brookes—"

"You *have* to remember me." Tears swelled and burned. "It's the *only* way we can go home."

This all happened because of Avalon's reckless ambition. Doing a story on a dark cult of sorcery was risky but Pulitzer Prize worthy. Unless Avalon got caught. Cursed. Trapped in an endless cycle of death with their husband. And their punishment was memory. Knowledge. Vivid clarity of what their lives used to be. The only escape was making Brighton see.

Desperate, Avalon tried something new and dove for a kiss. The second their lips touched the air crackled and sizzled. Charged. Electric.

A guard yanked Avalon away, slapping cuffs on them and hauling them to the gallows. Avalon struggled to look at Brighton.

"I promise!" they shouted, "I will get us out of here!"

Brighton, frozen, stared wide-eyed at them. The last thing Avalon saw was his baffled expression and a finger-graze across his lips.

AVALON WOKE WITH A SURPRISED GASP. A tingle on their lips. And Brighton, already at the cell, with fingers at his lips as well.

AGE CANNOT WITHER HER
BARBARA KRASNOFF (299 WORDS)

After her daughter closed the door behind her, Martha sat at her kitchen table and stared at the piece of paper in her hand. At 96, her memory had gotten so bad that she had to list all the things she had done that day or it was forgotten by the evening.

"We went over the bills," she wrote, knowing that it was her daughter who paid the bills that had piled up that week. "We made lunch," remembering the packages of frozen food that her daughter had brought for the coming week. "And we...."

"Oh, god," she cried out. "I've already forgotten everything."

"You haven't forgotten me," said Julia. She was perched on the kitchen windowsill, her feet in the sink. Her rich black hair was piled in elaborate braids around her head; her dark eyes crinkled with amusement.

Martha smiled despite herself. "I could never forget you," she said. Julia who was Martha's closest friend, maid of honor, and enthusiastic babysitter; Julia who stayed with Martha after her husband died and whose breast cancer killed her a year later. Was it already 20 years since that awful day?

"Don't look at me," Martha whispered. "I've gotten old. So old."

"Don't be ridiculous," said Julia. She still had the wondrous smile that always made Martha's heart race. "You're not old. Not the real you."

"I'm sorry," said Martha. "We could have. We should have."

Julia hopped down from the sink, took Martha's hand, and kissed her gently. "Screw could have," she said. "You've outgrown this place. Let's go. We've got eternities to explore."

Something in Martha broke open, and she suddenly felt clearer, more herself, than she had in years. She laughed, shrugged off her age and her humanity, and the two women went to find the future.

UPON REFLECTION
SHIRLEY MEIER (298 WORDS)

I hated mirrors. My reflection. A rib-showing skinny with ugly little pecs and stringy arms. Acne. Thin lips. A boy. I hated all that I saw. I'd cut that boy. Awkward.

I tried lipstick. Pink. Ugly, ugly, I scrawled all over the mirror. Then thought I was going crazy because my reflection started cleaning the mirror just a bit before I did, palms rubbing circles of soap a hair ahead of me. Steam fogging up the mirror as I tried to shower the ugly off my skin.

I'd get blood on the mirror when I cut myself. First shaving. Then to punish.

The night I was going to kill myself I ended up forehead and hands pressed to the cool, smooth surface, looked over. Hands pressed to cool and warming reflection separated by a shining glass line. My reflection had a semi-colon tattoo I didn't have; between my thumb and forefinger. I got that tattoo.

Hating, I shaved my head. Ratty dreads falling down. I stood in the bathroom, shivering, head down in the ring of dreadful hair, afraid to look. Afraid. I looked.

My reflection waved and, dancing up and down, pulled up on what turned out to be a lace-front wig, sleek black braids. Unsynched. She leaned forward and put her lips on the inside of the mirror, bronze-red not pink.

She was me. Wig. Lipstick. Eyelashes. I tried it. Shaking and sick. Dizzy. Beautiful. Me. I could finally see clearly what I'd missed for so long. She was me. Palm to palm. Lip to lip. Synchronized again.

I booked at the clinic. That was the day that the fog in the mirror cleared up for me. The fog of male, like steam after a shower, revealing. Clearly me.

I am the girl in the mirror.

GHOSTS
WARREN ROCHELLE (297 WORDS)

Honorable Mention

Russell stared at his hands. His fingers were translucent to the first joint. Ghost disease, stage 1. He hid them with skingloves, terrified someone would see, turn him in, and he'd wind up in the quarantine barracks, and never be seen again.

The skingloves worked for a few weeks, until stage 2, when white outlined his vanished fingers. Russell knew he could no longer hide from his husband. The white chafed and itched, making clothing impossible. He showed Theo his hands.

"Russ, how long?"

"Three weeks? I was afraid you'd run away or kick me out." At the shocked look on Theo's face, he stopped and kissed him. He didn't have enough words to explain his irrational fear.

"For better or worse, goofball." Theo laughed and kissed Russell back, held him, murmuring for always. That night they made love feverishly, fearful they had little time left. Afterwards, Theo kissed Russell's visible heart in his now-translucent Stage 2 chest.

Russell took sick leave. He kept away from windows and doors, as his body went from translucent to almost-transparent, Stage 3. In a week, his hands, his feet, his arms and legs. Nose, ears. The next week, thighs, back, the rest of his chest, nothing visible except his heart. He exuded heat. When the Ghost Friends network spread the word that the police were doing heat-seeking neighborhood sweeps, Russell begged Theo to go. Shaking his head, Theo held out his now-translucent hands.

Ghost Friends helped them escape to a sanctuary in the Blue Hills. There, they waited to be perfectly clear, the last stage. No longer dimmed by flesh, they would know each other in total clarity. Then, the two ghosts, warm whispers on the wind, would drift deep into green shadows and find the others haunting the woods.

IMPULSE
JAIME MUNN (300 WORDS)

Honorable Mention

The future is uncertain.

That's what it says on my tickertape fortune. Not that I rely on it to get through the morning, but it's still a weight on my narrow shoulders as I take a shower. The water silences outside noise but it can't drown my inner voices.

I throw a weave of silver over the glass walls, gaze into my own eyes soulfully. There are shadows slipping between shades of brown and a different face staring out from the pupils. My current personal demon, Estry.

Still potently present.

First law: a witch should never conjure a demon stronger than her own spirit. It's not that I never believed. It's just how can you rate your soul against a nebulous other? There are no scales.

She's stirring old memories alongside the echoes of past summonses; demons who'd left once my bidding was done. Estry isn't going.

Lights flicker in the bathroom. She's suddenly with me in more than possessing spirit. Her naked form pressing against me.

"You're the one holding onto me," she says.

Her voice is music. It stirs me in places where I've been numb for too long.

Pale skinned, Estry folds her arms around me—faux supportive—grinning at both of us in the mirrored glass. Dark and light. She's not my saviour. I know she's seducing me. Know I'm losing this battle. Not sure I even care enough to fight and that's scary!

She looks a lot like my ex. Demonic temptation. That's by design but I can't help being drawn in. My mind whispers: *if she goes, she's gone forever.*

I stare back. Feel the powerful warmth, the gentle touch. See the promise in her eyes.

It's all illusion.

It's not enough.

Surprising both of us, I banish her.

Certainty is a cold reward.

REFRACTION
GORDON BONNET (293 WORDS)

DIRECTOR'S CHOICE – J. Scott Coatsworth

Every day, Jase leaves the public pool building as I arrive. His auburn curls are still damp. We smile, say hi. That's it. I get there earlier, hoping at least to catch a glimpse while he's changing in the locker room, but no good. We pass, I swim, and spend the rest of the day dreaming about him, cursing my shyness.

Six weeks later, he makes the first move.

"Go for a walk, Liam?"

I return his flirty smile. "Sure. I can skip swimming today. I spend enough time in the water as it is."

"Me too." He laughs, and we turn toward Stewart Park. The weather is unsettled, dark clouds on the horizon, warm wind rising. We make awkward small talk. But when the first raindrop spatters my skin, he takes my hand. Our gazes lock. His eyes are sea-green, deep water you could lose yourself in.

"Don't be afraid. Whatever happens, stay with me."

The rain falls harder. It trickles down his face, leaving transparent streaks, like striations of glass following his contours. He undresses as the skies open up, finally standing on the sidewalk facing me, naked.

His body shimmers, crystalline, as the rain washes away his humanity. I look through him to the trees and the lake beyond.

"All water connects," he says. "Once you change, we can go anywhere together."

The force binding Jase's body vanishes, and he collapses into a puddle. Heart pounding, I kneel on the sidewalk, peer in. Beneath the surface, Jase's beautiful face looks up at me. Then a hand—clear as water—arcs out of the pool, grabs mine, pulls me in.

Floating, weightless. Our mouths meet, bodies entwine. Then he whispers in my ear, "Take a deep breath, Liam. It's faster that way."

Every year, I choose one of my favorite stories from the hundreds submitted to name my Director's Choice. This year, I had two that I just couldn't choose between. This is one of those stories–just beautiful and pure and sweet. It made my little gay heart sing...

–J. Scott Coatsworth, Director

LOVERS' LETTERS
GINGER STREUSEL (298 WORDS)

Honorable Mention

On Snap-Apple Night, little witches gather for fun and fortune-telling.

"Cut one long ribbon all the way around," Evie said, peeling a Red Delicious. "And chant, 'By this paring, let me discover the initials of my one true lover.' Now, throw the peel over your shoulder and see what letter it becomes."

"*S!*"

"I got *O!*"

"Miss Evie, what's yours?"

She looked down and sighed. "Mine's a *C.*" *Like always*. But Chris or Cat never came calling. "Go on, it's carving time." She waved them off to gossip amongst the pumpkins.

"Can *I* get a fortune-telling lesson?" Evie turned toward a familiar voice, deeper and richer than she remembered.

"Crispin! It's been *ages.*" He had a new name now, a stronger physique. Old softness had melted away, revealing a confident jaw and a big grin. "Seems like HRT is treating you well. Your arms are *huge!*" She hugged him tight. "You look great."

"You too, lovely." He squeezed her back, curly hair tickling her cheek. "So, about that lesson?"

Her heart fluttered like a fire-moth's wings. "We've peeled apples since we were kids. Did you forget how?"

"It's been a long time."

She offered him a pretty Pippin and a smile. "Not your namesake, but—"

"Close enough." He grinned back.

Evie guided him as he cut the winding peel. They chanted together, hearts and hands warmed by the magic. "Now toss it."

She stared, breathless, as it curled into an unmistakable green *E*.

Then it struck her: she'd never seen *his* lover's letter before.

"*Crisp*—" She met his eyes.

"It's always *E*. Is yours still—?"

"*Yes*, always." She held his newly scruffy face. "I loved you when I was Evan, and even more now that I'm Evie."

"Me too," he said, and kissed her forehead.

RUTI'S PRAYER
LLOYD A. MEEKER (297 WORDS)

Winner – First Place

Again Arum had not visited, let alone answered. Ruti's gift had been inadequate to attract the god as he passed by. Even though he was only an apprentice shaman, Ruti knew he'd felt Arum pass—the birds had stopped singing, and the breeze scampered through his wattle house as if the walls were made of bushes scrawny as his arms.

His prayer, that Tegon, the most beautiful warrior in the village, would return his love, love that made his whole body ache, remained unanswered. It seemed Arum required a finer gift than the smoke of sweetgrass rising on the song of his flute, but Ruti had nothing better to offer.

Tegon, whose teeth flashed when he smiled, whose glowing skin, streaked with sweat and dirt after wrestling made Ruti's tongue swell and drip to lick him clean. Tegon, who used him, then ignored him. Ruti put away his flute and left his house to bless the cooking fires.

At the fires, Tegon caught Ruti roughly by the arm. "Hold! Do you have a gift for me today? I give you my beautiful cock to suck, but you give me nothing." He laughed, a sound with barbed edges. "Your flute has made your lips strong. If you really loved me you would give me your flute as a gift."

In a blink, Ruti could see into the man laughing at him. Beneath the beautiful flesh a demon-shadow nestled around his heart, chewing. The god had answered his prayer with truth: Tegon would never love him—or anyone. Arum's love called to him. Arum would respect Ruti's love.

He smiled, a little sad but freed by the vision. "No," Ruti said. "The flute is not mine to give. I just carry it, and its music belongs only to Arum."

What a unique, well-written little fantasy tale, sexy and sharp. The judges chose this one for its strong character voice and clever use of theme.

ORANGE DUST
NICOLE DENNIS (300 WORDS)

My reflection in the window was despised. A desiccated husk trapped in a wheelchair. My blue eyes bright and sharp. My mind crystal clear. The Orange Dust Disease is killing me. Slowly.

"Let us enter! He's a victim."

With one finger on controls, I spun my chair.

"Antony, I'm your twin, Maxim. They separated us, but I found you." My replica crouched near me. Another man stood behind him.

"You can't take him," a doctor ordered.

"We read the files. He followed his partner to the student protest, but left him."

Memories raced through me. I couldn't stay within the crowd. Disappointment shadowed my partner's face. I failed him. Again. Clarity hit me. This was it. We were no more. I walked away.

"He wasn't by the Chancellor's palace when the military released the orange dust, but in the eastern piazza. The dust dissipated, caused a slower reaction, and why he lives. It's why you want to keep him. For experiments and tests."

My mind flipped back to that day. Student's chants filtered through the streets. A voice on a bullhorn warned them. Orange dust floated along the streets. The regime's deadly response. In agony for two years, my partner died. I lingered for ten years.

"Does he know about the cure?"

My eyes widened. *Cure?*

"Antony, there is a cure to the orange dust. Liam helped discover it." Maxim smiled at his partner. "We can restore most of you, but not the chair. Do you want this? Blink twice for yes. Three for no."

Blinked twice. Paused. Blinked twice.

Maxim moved behind my chair. "We're taking him away. The regime is falling. He's not your prisoner."

A window flickered from dark to clear. I glanced at my reflection. With clarity, I knew I would never see this image again.

WILLOWS
AMANDA MEUWISSEN (300 WORDS)

Bran knew now that fae weren't merely mischievous beings who granted favors. The old stories were the real ones, warning of friendly and malicious fae alike, because they were all the same.

One could never tread on fae lands without consequence.

They were fierce, just the wrong side of beautiful and unsettling to look at for too long. Small, large, waiflike, bulbous, horned, fanged, winged, all kinds, all colors, and they descended like a ravenous pack of wolves.

Bran remained in the grip of the dryads, arms locked behind his back in the knots of their trunks, as the fair folk dragged Shia away. Screaming and clawing at the ground, Shia looked so fragile, when only moments prior he had been safe in Bran's arms after a stolen kiss beneath the willows.

Shia's screams grew worse once Bran could no longer see him, echoing howls and then... gurgles, until the noises stopped. This was Bran's fault for suggesting a shortcut, for wanting to look for fae like he had as a child.

Fae take wicked boys, Bran's mother used to warn, but he wasn't a boy anymore, and he'd long since stopped believing that yearning for the young man he met in the woods made him wicked.

Then Shia came into the light, monochrome in red-black blood, and none of it was his. His eyes shined like emeralds, skin almost iridescent, ears pointed, and body moving like liquid seeping along a fissure.

He waved a hand, and the dryads burst into ashes, releasing Bran's arms, and causing him to flail backward.

Shia approached and held out a bloody hand. "You're safe with me."

Bran knew not to trust fae. He knew now how true the old stories were.

But maybe there was good among the wicked.

He took Shia's hand.

IF THE SHOE FITS
SI CLARKE (299 WORDS)

The seer sweeps into the room and takes a seat. 'You had an interesting conversation yesterday.'

I roll my eyes. 'Be more specific. I met seventy-eight people yesterday. Did you know that? Do you care?'

'The engineer.'

Unexpected. 'Them? Really?'

'All will become clear,' says the seer in that condescending, infuriating way. 'Tell me.'

✥

THE ENGINEER ACCEPTED the proffered shoe with a cynical grin. 'What the hell good is a glass shoe?'

I sighed. How humiliating. 'Believe me, I know. My seer – well, *the* seer – anyway, it's supposed to lead me to…' I must've descended to muttering after that because they chuckled.

'Sorry? Couldn't make that last bit out.'

I coughed and looked away. I hated the seer for making me do this. 'It's supposed to lead me to the, er, the chosen one.'

The engineer peered into the shoe, inspecting it – possibly trying to suppress a grin. 'How's it work, then?'

✥

THE SEER INTERRUPTS MY STORY. 'They didn't try it on?'

I glare at the seer. 'They did *not* put the ridiculous shoe on. At no point in the conversation did the engineer put the shoe on. I pressed a hand to my forehead, massaging my temples – much like I'm doing now, you'll notice – and said, "No idea. Honestly, this is really embarrassing."'

The seer looks me in the eye – stares into my soul, more like. 'You didn't suggest they try it on?'

'I'm coming to that. "Most people just try it on, to be honest," I said.'

The seer's eyebrows lift. 'And they still didn't?'

'Nope. Just looked at me and asked "Why?"'

'Nothing else?'

I lean back in my wheelchair. 'And then they answered, "Pretty stupid way for a country to choose its leader – don't you think?"'

The seer smiles. 'We've found the one.'

ARENE, 27F, INVISIBLE
A. B. ENCARNACION (299 WORDS)

Honorable Mention

The "career" field seems the best place to confess it. She tries to set expectations, luring matches with the novelty of dating someone you don't need to make eye contact with—but when the first beer empties, smiles unravel.

I can't believe you're actually...

Her dates search, squinting.

But, are you actually a...?

"Yes," Arene replies, and leaves if they persist, wanting her to confirm breasts beneath her sweater. She tries a flower hairpin, sun-shaped earrings, a dress that doesn't stop someone from mashing his fingertips into the chest cutout. Even when her closet swells too full to shut, nothing in it stops her dates from startling at her voice. *Oh,* a woman stammers once, *it—sounds different from an invisible throat,* but growing up this way makes you perceive everything that isn't obvious: she wasn't expecting the accent.

"Filipino!" Arene hears one day, and she sputters. This new date laughs, which means Arene's gape is evident by some trailing droplet.

"I'm hard to place too," they offer. "I'm half. Call me Siya."

"Oh," Arene says, because they can't see her smiling. "I get it."

It's the first time she gets past happy hour without feeling like someone's watching the food mash in her mouth, the first time she laughs unintentionally, the first time her hand indents the lines of an outstretched palm.

It's raining. They leave together, running to Siya's apartment, soaked, her heart pounding so hard she'd be afraid of its obviousness, if she hadn't for years feared it wasn't there at all. They fumble at the door, laughing, and Arene unpeels her layers, coat shirt underwear everything. Siya kisses her, without missing, and later they say it was easy: her lips and lashes and throat were beaded by rain, and light shone all through her, prismatic.

SCIENCE FICTION PART ONE

I am sweating as I look at the twelve faces, though I shouldn't be nervous: I've done nothing wrong, but I've never trusted these chambers. They must make mistakes, like the polygraph tests from centuries ago, though the experts say they're flawless.

— NATHAN ALLING LONG, *THE SHADOW OF DOUBT*

POST-APOCALYPTIC GOO
DEVON WIDMER (300 WORDS)

Kit rummaged through the rubble of what had once been Mr. Miller's house.

Mean Mr. Miller. The English teacher who'd made Kit's first semester of high school hell. Still, despite his bad temper, he'd always managed to get Kit's pronouns right: ey/em.

Mr. Miller hadn't deserved this. None of them had.

The ding of a bicycle bell sounded from the nearby pavement.

Kit glanced up. Stephanie Bandini. Lakefield High Freshman Class President, 2019. Lakefield Post-Apocalyptic Commune President, 2020. Ever since everyone over the age of sixteen had inexplicably detonated at the dawn of the new year, teens like Stephanie and Kit had become the town's greatest authorities.

Stephanie rolled her eyes. "Don't tell me you're looking for *goo* again."

Kit shrugged and turned eir attention back to eir work. Ey liked Stephanie. She didn't leave anyone behind—even the loners like Kit who hadn't joined the commune.

But Kit had a broader definition of "no one left behind."

As the clatter of Stephanie's rusty bicycle receded into the distance, Kit turned over a crumbling patch of drywall.

There it was: a splatter of murky blue.

BACK AT EIR FARM, Kit strained the goo, extracting every speck of debris, until it sparkled clear as the blue sky.

After placing the goo in a clean jar, Kit whistled, long and steady. As the note faded from the air, silence fell upon the farm. Silence and stillness.

Then, motion. Rustling. Oozing. Goo emerged from secret napping spots, from secret sunning spots, from secret goo meetings and secret goo solitude. A rainbow of goo gathered at Kit's feet, tittering curiously at the jar of what had once been Mr. Miller.

The goo in the jar rippled and gurgled. It drew its mass inward, then upward, rising out of the jar and into its community.

BATHTUB GIN
ANDREA STANET (299 WORDS)

Basil reached into the claw-foot bathtub and scooped up a mason jar full of the purest, clearest liquid he'd made in all his time of moonshining. He held it up to the night sky, sprinkled liberally with early summer constellations. A fat moon beamed down.

"May the goddess's light illuminate the drinker's true heart to transparency that their radiance and beauty are visible to all, drawing to them the love they desire." Pierre chanted.

"As spirit wills," Basil responded.

The enchanted hooch inside the jar shimmered bright blue and then continued to sparkle subtly in the moonlight. Basil capped the potion—the last one for the night, reserved for Miss Miranda who had her eye on the new railway clerk.

Basil pulled on his clothes—tan striped brown pants as dark as his skin and an untucked white shirt. A top hat perched on woolly curls. He picked up his crow's head cane, waved it over the tub, and watched a crackle of blue energy zap it and the distillery back into the cellar.

By the time he finished dressing, Pierre had his clothes on with a lightning pistol strapped to his thigh. One never knew when the coppers might show. Goggles sat atop the brim of his bowler, and a thick leather greave with potion-filled cartridges covered one sepia arm. His other was held out, patiently waiting to be clasped.

Their fingers intertwined.

"That batch is strong, love. Strongest we've made, I think," Basil said.

"Yes, I felt that! Miss Miranda will be pleased. Mayhaps we'll be invited to another wedding before winter solstice."

Basil chuckled. "And get some new referrals for folks needing a touch of help being *seen*."

Arms hooking around each other's waists, the two mages climbed the steps of their cabin in the woods.

IMPACT
SAGE HN (298 WORDS)

Eight seconds to impact.

The computer's voice counts down the seconds left in my life, cold. My spaceship is surrounded by battle, shrapnel spangling the fold of space. I'm trapped, no way out.

Seven seconds.

The general said true love would save us in our darkest hour. But I don't have that luxury. My darkest hour is here, and I have nothing to show for it but my busted ship and the countdown ticking ever closer to zero.

Six seconds.

I could cry, but tears won't save me.

Five seconds to impact.

My commander always told us to hold on to something life-sized. Something at home that we could fight for, when the rest of the world seemed too big.

But I'm fat, and I'm femme, and I'm aroace, Arab and queer, and the world I lived in never loved me. So how could I find something I loved enough to come back for?

Four seconds.

I could say I loved Emmeline, or Lora, or Safia, or Rima. I could say I loved Noor and Rin and Alex to pieces, but none of it would mean anything to the people in power. Maybe love doesn't discriminate, but the people who control it do.

Three seconds.

I don't want to die here.

Two seconds.

I think of warm brown eyes and a soft brown body. I think of her yellow hijab embroidered with flowers. *Come back to me,* she seems to say. But I can't. Can't I?

One second to impact.

I love her, I realize. Not romantically, and not as a friend. As... my person. Realization settles in me, cold and clear as dawn.

Impact detect...e...d

My ship bursts apart, but I am gone on a wink, a dream, to my soft brown girl who feels like home.

OYSTERS AND OTHER SLIMY CREATURES
ALLAN DYEN-SHAPIRO (300 WORDS)

Kwame Jackson's fourth graders fidgeted. The sun was hot; the benches, uncomfortable. Already in bathing suits, they longed to splash in Tampa Bay's warm water.

Not Sarah. She raised her hand to ask Gregory Xiao still another question. "Wikipedia's oyster-reef-restoration article said old shells worked for cultch. Why do we need your company's stuff?"

She'd likely looked up the word cultch before the field trip to show off, but attention-seeking engendering learning worked for Kwame. Besides, it gave Kwame an excuse to focus on the shirtless Gregory Xiao. His powerful arms glistened with perspiration. How wonderful it would be if they held Kwame against Gregory's near-hairless chest.

"Xiao Biotech's recombinant proteins buffer the water's pH near the cultch. The larvae that settle make shells just like before ocean acidification. Oysters maturing on the beds we build today will filter the water, so the sun can shine on the seagrass, and healthy seagrass will feed manatees." Gregory grinned sheepishly. "Did this make sense?"

Sarah assured him it did.

Mesmerized by Gregory's melodious voice, Kwame couldn't say but assumed so.

"Good. Let's get started." Gregory beckoned, and the children followed.

Upon reaching the water, Sarah pointed to a brown plume near the brand-new hotel. "What's that?"

"It's what the oysters filter. No water clarity without oysters. Sorry, kids —we'll reschedule."

Sarah sniffed the air. "It's poop."

"Sewage. My father's resort has a release permit."

Gregory Xiao, Xiao Biotech, Xiao Resorts. Gregory's father also owned politicians. Kwame choked back an urge to vomit.

Later, when Kwame had the children onto the bus, Gregory smiled seductively and proffered a pen. "You're gorgeous," he whispered over the bus's motor. "Can I have your number?"

The oysters hadn't achieved clarity, but Kwame had. "No." He stepped onto the bus and shut the door in Gregory's face.

CYCLES
SCOTT JENSON (296 WORDS)

I signaled the instructor that I had a question.

They nodded to me.

I transmitted to the class. "Instructor Rivers, why do some become parents and others do not?"

Instructor emoted amusement. "All consummate children, but not all will conduct the Parenting. Would you want to be the one to parent?"

I furrowed my brow.

During the rest of the lessons, I questioned my wanting.

The Attention-Minder sent my instructors notice for my lack of attention as I left the lesson hall.

Quickly followed by the Health-Minder signaling for me to go to medical.

The lift took me across Nibru station overlooking the bright reflection of Sol on Jupiter, lighting up the modules of the station colony. The black of the solar system's sky hung stars and dancing miners and transports heading in-system or out-system.

A Health-Minder Drone greeted me at the lift. "Hello, our system registered you as having entered the phase of Questioning. Are you ready to experience the choice?"

I worried at my cheek. "Can you make the wrong choice?"

Health-Minder flashed green and red. "You can change, and the choice selected that is correct now may not be years from now. There are no right fits that do not include growth and change."

We entered the clinic.

I sat on the indicated chair. "How do you find the right cycle?"

Health-Minder had me lay back, answering, "We have years of data on your body and mind. We project likely growth patterns for both your body's and mind's needs, and you pick the cycle best suited to you. Male, Female, or between."

The scanner moved around my head and over my body. "What if I never want, or nobody wants what I choose?"

Health-minder signaled calm. "Community-Minder will assist in your future partnerings."

THE BEST SOLUTION
DAVID VINER (297 WORDS)

The glass doors swished open and Clarice entered. One wall of the waiting room proclaimed "Perspicuity Life Solutions Inc." in huge lettering. Clarice was the only one there.

"Damn him," she hissed, seating herself. "Damn all men."

She'd dissolved their contract on the commute into work, knowing she was now effectively homeless. "Maybe I can kip on Lexi's sofa."

She'd made the appointment during morning break. A cancellation had freed the 17:30 slot, so she'd grabbed it.

"Clarice Heidrun, room five."

The announcement made her jump. She stood, heading for the door that swung open as she approached.

"Please take a seat, Ms Heidrun," said the girl, smiling, indicating a chair in front of the apparatus. "My name's Lucida Kailash. First time?"

Clarice nodded, noticing how the pupils of Lucida's eyes dilated as their eyes met. *Damn, she's pretty.*

"Please sign this waiver. It gives us permission to rummage through your brain. Don't worry, the data's automatically deleted upon completion."

Clarice signed.

Lucida secured the headset to Clarice's skull.

"What's it do, exactly?"

"Identifies and analyses your life issues. Then it seeks the optimal remediation."

"How long will it take?"

"About ten minutes."

"Oh, that quick."

"Ready?"

"Yes."

Lucida typed on her keyboard and Clarice's head tingled. Random lights and almost forgotten memories flashed across her mind. Nine minutes passed before they stopped.

"All finished," Lucida announced, removing the headset. She stared at her screen. "Right, what have we got here? Ah, the usual life troubles. Ooh, lots of man issues, and oh…"

"Oh?"

"Well... that's a new one."

"Is there a problem?"

"Um… depends. Apparently, the best solution for your life circumstances is…"

"What?"

"Me," Lucida gulped.

Their eyes met once more – the moment lasted forever.

"Not a problem," Clarice whispered.

Lucida smiled, "No, clearly not."

THE SHADOW OF DOUBT
NATHAN ALLING LONG (300 WORDS)

I am staring at my jury—six men and six women—from inside the truth chamber, which looks more like a giant crystal placed in the middle of the court room. I'm not sure how it works, but somehow only completely truthful statements can be heard by those outside the chamber—any lie I say remains trapped within these glass walls for me alone to hear.

I am sweating as I look at the twelve faces, though I shouldn't be nervous: I've done nothing wrong, but I've never trusted these chambers. They must make mistakes, like the polygraph tests from centuries ago, though the experts say they're flawless.

"Mr. Alling, did you murder Manuel Dito?" the prosecutor asks me point blank.

"No," I say.

"Full sentence please," she replies.

"No, I didn't murder Manuel Dito." I look at the jury, who have clearly heard my words, but I feel compelled to say more, to convince them beyond a shadow of doubt. "I've never murdered anyone," I said. "I'm an innocent man."

The prosecutor turns suddenly. "What was the last thing you said? We didn't hear it."

"I'm innocent," I said.

She nods her head. "We heard it that time," she says. "Very well then."

The jury smiles at me as I step out of the chamber. I want to believe I've just proven the truth chamber fallible, but I do not protest it. I do not say a word.

I feel something tight grow inside me, a silent seed I've always sensed was there. As I walk out of the courtroom, it unfurls so rapidly, I can no longer hold it back or press it down. I know I must investigate it fully, the truth I've been hiding all these years: I am innocent, but I am not a man.

BLUE
KAYLEIGH SKY (299 WORDS)

Not sky blue. Not cornflower blue. Not robin's egg blue. Not cerulean, sapphire, or topaz.

"Ice," he thinks.

He can't tear his gaze away, frozen in the blue pools staring back at him.

A memory surfaces. Sitting at Matt's bedside, breaths away from losing him, hiding from the mobs outside. The crazies hunting water. They'd shot Matt and ransacked the house. Stolen their last stores of Crystal Geyser. Stale and brackish, but water. He'd found the anniversary-trip brochure searching for any stray bottles, sat at Matt's side, trifold trembling in his fingers.

Matt had coughed a whisper-dry chuckle. "We missed the boat."

The cruise of a lifetime. But only because…

Everything was dying.

Last chance to see an iceberg.

They should have cared more. Shouldn't have counted on the desalination plants. On the power grid.

A day later, he'd buried Matt with the brochure, the shouting mobs far away.

Everything is clearer in a rearview mirror. Crystalline, at the end. Clear as the blue gaze holding his.

How long could he last?

No matter. He wanted only to be with Matt again, warm in his arms, skin soft and plump with water.

Water as clear and blue as ice. As blue as the stare fixed on his. Wondrous irises, fissured and fractured in layers, vast as the galaxy, bottomless as the long ago seas.

Fresh, sweet, wasted, gone.

Clarity is as sharp as an icicle, as withering as the wind off an ice field, flaying skin off the lasting bones.

As blue as the planet spinning eternally.

He rasps, "What are you?"

It crackles, "You."

Of course.

The eyes in the mirror are as blue as ice, as clear as the lakes and seas that are no more, as finite and fragile as the stars shining their dead light.

MEET ME AT THE SOUTH GATE
ALMA NILSSOM (299 WORDS)

I read her message again.
Meet me at the South Gate.
I wait.

Around me, nervous singletons also wait. Military males fresh off their starships in their smart black uniforms. I'm one of the few females here. I could be meeting a husband-to-be.

But I'm not.

My nervous hands straighten invisible wrinkles.

I see her coming down the pedestrian street. Brightly colored shoes among all the black ones. Her human skin is the color of the sky at sunset, and her eyes are the color of the leaves during the spring. Human. She is nothing like me; she is alien.

She smiles at me from a distance.

I don't return her smile. I only smile when I'm embarrassed. My right hand adjusts my braided hair, so it falls down attractively over my left shoulder, showing off the silver jewelry I chose, especially for meeting her here today. This place where only serious lovers meet.

"Humans are always late," I say when she's close enough. She smells of nectarines and jasmine. I breathe her in and notice I can hardly hear my own words because of my deafening heartbeat.

She sweetly purses her pink lips, "Well, it's not as easy for me to navigate an alien megacity, my friend."

"Shall we go in?" I gesture to the South Gate. A few rogue purple blossoms have escaped and are floating on the wind around us.

She doesn't answer. Instead, she looks around, noticing the males in their uniforms inspecting us with more than curiosity in their eyes. I shouldn't use my telepathic skills as it's forbidden, but I must know what's going through her human mind.

A quick sweep, and my heart is singing. She knew this was the romantic gate to meet, and this was not merely a human mistake.

SAD REALITY
STEPHEN B. PEARL (298 WORDS)

Jason leaned against the wall of the space elevator transfer station. For the sake of his friend, his love, he fought not to cry. Bill stood on the other side of the space dock, clutching an attractive dark-haired woman. A pair of children hugged them both around the legs. For two years, those lips had been Jason's to kiss, those hands his to hold.

When the accident happened, they'd been friendly colleagues. Then two years of uncertainty. Communications cut off. Not sure at any moment if a survival critical system would give out. It was only luck that the drive component failed on the return trajectory of their mission. They'd tweaked their course enough for the slow drift back to Earth. Then had come the waiting.

At first, the touching had been a way to remember they were alive. The sex had come later to fend off boredom and remove stress. The love had grown next. Two years of loving and being loved, but he'd known it was over the day they re-established communications with Earth. The day Susan's face appeared on the viewscreen, astounded that her husband was returned from the grave.

After that, Sue had loomed over Bill when they made love. A distance had grown between the lovers despite their small living space.

Jason sighed. Clarity could hurt. He had loved a straight man that circumstances gave him for a pair of years. It was clear that to speak of what they had been to each other would harm his beloved in ways that could shatter four lives.

Bill caught Jason's eyes with his own. Bill smiled and mouthed the words, thank you. There would be more words, as friends, in the years to come, and it was clear that would have to be enough.

HARMONY
JAYMIE WAGNER (298 WORDS)

JUDGE'S CHOICE – Angel Martinez

They were drowning in inescapable noise.
   Jr jrypbzr lbh gb bhefryirf bhe ubzr bhe zvaq bhe jbeyq bhe fbhy!
   Why (Orpnhfr) did (you) I (jrer) do (arrqrq) this?
   Jr pna fubj lbh. Yrg hf uryc you/hf.
   They found a life preserver floating on the chaos. Clinging desperately to it, pulled along by the current.
   Cyrnfr fgbc svtugvat hf / you / nyy. Wbva gur sybj. Yrg it svyy you. Let us fcrnx.
   Memories of the smell of black coffee in sterile station air.
   Yes. Erzrzore. Let guvf guide you. Uryc us haqrefgnaq you.
   "You don't have to," the Secretary said, his office window showcasing the slowly turning planet beneath them. "This whole thing is...a lot."
   "But...?"
   You were gur bayl one.
   "The simulation scores and test results don't lie. You're our best candidate by a wide margin, but even if it works there's no guarantee of coming back."
   Jr jbhyq zvff You ohg we jbhyq yrg you tb, if you jvfurq to yrnir.
   But if it worked, it would be something beautiful.
   Rira orsber you Xarj us you haqrefgbbq.
   "Sir, I'm in."
   The memory faded, used to transform the life preserver into a boat to navigate the current. An understanding that shaped the cacophony into beautiful song.

You ner doing jryy! We are here - we are nqncgvat. Pbzr, you are so pybfr.

Joy intertwined with acceptance and curiosity. Carefully retaining themselves but now part of this branching, beautiful network, so beautiful in its complexity.

Yes! Yes, we/you frr us! You see!

AS THEIR EYES OPENED, Yia could see the beautiful translucent wings of the Bynthei who had overseen their attempt to join the (*oversoul*) fluttering with delight.

Hello, they thought. *I am Yia, the ambassador from the Free Republic. My pronouns are they/them.*

Welcome, Yia-Ambassador.

Welcome home.

Stories that take risks tend to catch my attention, and Harmony certainly does that. The author cleverly illustrates humans attempting to communicate with an alien collective, but the humans need someone who thinks differently for any chance of success. Both a metaphor for the rewards of communicating with someone on their own terms and for the ways in which thinking beyond the binary can expand our universe, this story packs a lot of meaning into less than three hundred words.

By the end, the story wraps us in warmth and inclusion. Lovely and well-crafted, this story will stay with me as a bright spot of time.

—Angel Martinez

THE TRUTH SAYER
CARO SOLES (292 WORDS)

I would remember this moment forever. I could barely see him at first, standing by the hatch that was not supposed to be opened. A large, loose-limbed Terran male, all darting eyes and big careless feet and hands that looked like shovels. I wondered what those hands would feel like on me. But I was not supposed to think like that. I was promised. At that moment I didn't care. I didn't care about the rituals and the oaths. the proud parents, the jealous siblings. I didn't want all that anymore, I wanted him.

I knew next to nothing about Terrans except there were two sexes and usually one wanted the other. I was both in one body. Untouched. Yearning. Would that do? I stepped out into the light.

He caught his breath and his mouth quirked up in a tentative smile. "You're a Truth Sayer."

"I can't tell you my name," I said, and I reached out to touch his arm and then I felt it, his feelings, his deep desire, his uncertainty. He was much younger than I had thought. I breathed in the rank boy smell of him, the energy held in check, the desire spreading out like a searchlight to see if I could satisfy this hunger.

"I better go," he said, but I knew he didn't want to. Not without an answer.

I moved closer, still holding onto his arm. "For you I am all male. Touch me and you will know the answer."

His long fingers were hot against my skin and for a moment I was frightened by the kind of tingling contact I had never experienced. But I craved him like my next breath. This was my truth. I was giving it to him.

COLD CONVICTION
JENNIFER HASKIN (291 WORDS)

You know all those stories about post-apocalyptic destruction, right? In every scenario, whether climate disaster, nuclear winter, or some other worldwide tragedy we inflict on ourselves, the end result is always the same. We all die. But, and there's a big irony here folks, we actually don't.

Oh, we were so wrapped up in pronoun political war that we never saw the nuke coming. I mean, really. If you don't like what I call myself, then don't call me anything. Please. Just don't.

Just as they'd predicted forever, nuclear winter is shit. Luckily, at the price of your identity and freedom, one could "buy" a living space in a billionaire bunker. While we were bickering about what's in whose pants, the elite of the country were merely playing idiots and had each invested in a company called iBunk. I know, stupid or cliché? You pick.

They had built vast complex cities underground. They knew it was only a matter of time. They knew if they diverted power to their underground cities, life would go on as it always had. Another new normal. One they owned—as gods. Giving them my identity was hard, my freedom harder.

Those who didn't pay, aren't here anymore. But wherever they exist, they are free. Forever. A thing I will never be. Never see the sky on my own planet, never breathe fresh open air, never watch the moon, feel the sun on my face again. Never eat when or what I choose, never sleep in, never have a day off, never *own* my things, my money, or my life. Maybe if I had stopped—if I could have imagined the price of the prison I was entering before panic set in—I'd be free too.

HEARTSBEATS
JENDAYI BROOKS-FLEMISTER (291 WORDS)

Honorable Mention

I pull my fingers out of you. Our heavy breathing is synchronized, low and animalistic. I unhook the strap and go to the sink to rinse my hands and toy of the beautiful mess that is your orgasm. It's our sixth date and the fourth time we've ended it in bed. My eyes drift along your sweaty honey-brown skin, your breasts heaving from our mutual workout. I look from your body to the window, where I see the stars or planets or satellites or aliens dancing in the familiar void above. For the first time, I wonder if I should finally tell you.

"You know, maybe we should make this official," you say.

My hearts are dancing in my chest. A relationship with you? Stability. Safety. I crave it more than you'll ever know. But I can't give it to you. Not yet. Not with so much unsaid. How can I explain how I got here, who I am? How can I explain my fascination with this planet and its people, which led me to the club which led me to you? How can I make it clear that I'm not a threat, that I'm here to stay for *you*? My brain is so muddled it almost hurts.

"I need to tell you something," I blurt out. You *need* to know.

You stand and approach me, each step rippling up your thighs. You stop just inches from my face, your breath still heavy with my pleasure. You rest your head on my chest. I can feel your heart fluttering against my skin. Your index and middle fingers tap against my chest in a quick, consistent rhythm. In time with my hearts. It hits me.

"I know," you say. "I've always known."

PARANORMAL

Your teeth close around my throat. We've wrestled a hundred times, play-fighting until you slip and go wolf. But as your wolf-eyes meet mine, there's something new in their depths.

— KAJE HARPER, *BENEATH THE SURFACE*

A GREY MAN
TERRY POOLE (297 WORDS)

No one sees me. No one cares as I sit alone.

I am the ultimate Grey Man, completely invisible.

Do I have any regrets? No.

Maybe one.

I never got the chance to say goodbye to the one who was lost to me a long ago.

My time will eventually come as it does to all living things. I wonder if I will see him again. Is there really a Heaven?

"Daniel?"

The name shakes me out of my thoughts, and I glance up.

It's not possible? It can't be!

"C – Chris?" My voice rough from lack of use.

He smiles down at me and holds out his hand. I stare at it in confusion before meeting his gaze once more. The green eyes that have haunted my dreams for years are just as bright as I remember. Soft and full of love – for me.

It's like the sun has risen for the first time in forever coating Chris in a bright halo.

"How?"

Chris continues to smile. "I've missed you."

"I -"

"Take my hand, Daniel."

I don't question him, staring at his beloved face as I take the offered hand and rise to my feet. His hand is warm as mine envelopes his.

"It's time for you to join me."

Chris tugs on my hand and I follow him. He leads me towards the sun, and I pause. The urge to look behind me is overwhelming and I glance over my shoulder.

I'm still sitting in my wheelchair unseen, unnoticed. It looks like I'm sleeping.

"Don't worry, my love. Everything will be fine. Better than fine. We will be together and that's enough."

He's right. I squeeze his hand and he squeezes back. I have my answer now and we walk side-by-side into the light.

THE GLIMPSE
ANNE SMITH (292 WORDS)

Honorable Mention

In the mirror, I slit my throat. I don't know why. Someone else is guiding my hand, and while I cannot see them, I feel the warmth of their touch. My reflection changes each time, and I bring my fingers up to my face to feel my skin shift.

My face morphs into the little boy, the little boy whose mother had a suit tailored for his eighth-grade graduation, and he tugs fruitlessly at the sleeves and the collar in hot anguish. His face is childishly tired, a glow in his eyes with nowhere to put it.

The blood recedes like a rewinding cassette. I slit my throat again.

My fingers catch, this time, the cracking of my nose. A rebellious teenage girl, hair dip-dyed blue in future regrets; my teeth contort to accommodate her jagged smile. She seems happier, in an angry way, the way that people sneer at. She will listen to rock that others call 'too pop' and break her wrist punching a wall. She cannot wear skirts, but she's a teenage girl still.

The blood drifts back, stitching my throat together. I slit it again.

I smile at the old woman in the mirror. She seems nice; she smells like dirt and overwhelming lavender perfume, and her skin sags in that gorgeous manner. Her hair is falling out and her floral dress is marked in mismatched seams and patches. I feel every vertebra in my back crumble, but I gratefully exchange this youth for a modicum of her peace.

The blood returns to my body; the warmth of the hand vanishes as quickly as it came. I hold the cold razor to my throat, before placing it back on the dresser. I loosen my tie, unbuttoning my collar.

THE GHOST MAID
CRYSTA K. COBURN (298 WORDS)

Harmony sat in half lotus, hands in gyan mudra. The house groaned in the wind. She'd grown accustomed to the usual sounds in previous visits; when the owners recited to her the legend.

A married couple once lived there with their maid, who fell in love with the husband. She shot him in jealousy. He grabbed the gun and shot her dead in the parlor, where Harmony sat.

The tale's simplicity would have made Harmony doubt its veracity if she hadn't felt the maid's spirit. At the close of the telling, she'd come forward, wailing, shaking windowpanes. Only Harmony saw her. The others merely shivered at the sudden cold.

The cold, disembodied footsteps, and misbehaving electricity kept people from inhabiting the house. Harmony sensed the spirit's profound loneliness. Why scare people away when you wished them near?

Night descended. Still she waited, inviting the spirit to appear. The room grew cold. The spirit gathered before Harmony.

"Why are you sad? D'you miss your lover?"

The maid sobbed.

"He's gone."

She shook her head furiously, wailing. Harmony felt she'd said something wrong.

"Are you glad he's gone?"

The spirit sighed, nodded.

"You're lonely. You miss someone."

The room's shadows took form, showing three figures. Two smaller figures huddled together. A large shadow loomed above, then wrestled with one of the smaller ones. *Pop—pop—pop!* The small shadow fell away. The large grabbed the other small one, and all three disappeared.

"You didn't love him. But you were in love."

She bowed low in relief. Harmony understood.

"You were in love with her. He killed you when he discovered you together."

Shaking with sobs, she nodded.

"She must be waiting. I'll tell everyone your real story. You can rest now."

The spirit held her hands in thanks, then dissipated.

NEVER ALONE
RIN SPARROW (300 WORDS)

Honorable Mention

My mind was mud. As obscure and murky as the dirt and clay seeping between my toes. The smell of the wet forest enveloped me as rain ran down my naked body.

This was my Day of Ascension. The first male shifter to become Shaman in two generations. But when I shifted before them, they would see. My shifter fox was female.

No one knew, save one.

"I know you're there, Ahu."

Out from the trees came a lynx.

"What are you doing here?"

"What are *you* doing here? The Elders wait in the clearing. Yet here you stand. Human."

"You don't understand."

"I wouldn't." She shrugged as much as her shoulders allowed. "Perhaps the Ancestors can give answers." Turning, she called, "See you in the morning, Pasha." She still used the childish name for me. Annoying. Comforting.

Breathing slowly, I sat in the soaked mud and shut my eyes.

Immediately, I plummeted. The nether realm greeted me as I opened my eyes. From the mist, a swallow descended. "You come. But alone."

I knew her voice. We had communed before.

"A swamp idles within me."

She chirped impatiently. "You question your role, for your people?"

"No... Much has been made of a male Shaman ascending, yet..."

"You are not always that."

"No."

She shifted to a snow-white leopard. Only Spirits could be so mercurial. Her gaze met mine, Intense. Piercing.

"History is long. You think you are the first?"

Others appeared about us. Wolves. Leopards. Lemurs.

"You are Blessed as the bridge between two worlds. Spirit and man. Even male and female."

My breath hitched as understanding dawned. I was not cursed to abolishment or abandonment.

Blessed.

Embracing her, I guided the Spirits within, and I opened my eyes to the world.

I stood. Head clear.

It was time.

VERITY
JULIE BOZZA (278 WORDS)

Her mind was clear, but the rest of her barely existed at all; she was translucent at best, when in life she'd been bold enough to write her own indelible truths. Of course, by the time her pen's ink on paper became printer's ink within books, these truths were somewhat diluted...

So, she should be used to it, really. She shouldn't be surprised to see her darling Stella described as her "boon companion" or her "bosom friend", or her pious "helpmeet". Even the latest biography, which claimed to be daring, settled for "life partner" – and then skated over the full implications with an "Of course we can't *know*...". Daring, indeed!

And she couldn't do anything about it. Black ink on white paper might prove fragile in the living world; might be ephemeral, hidden, or obscured. But for her the marks made were solid and immutable.

Until eventually an age dawned in which her Stella-star could have become her lawfully wedded wife. Among other such wonders was an encyclopedia composed entirely of light and electricity... After some experimentation on these newfangled pixels, she discovered that at last she could actually *do* something.

Slowly, one by one, readers awoke to see the words "her love, her lover, Stella" and some even followed the reference to "manuscripts in trunk, Thornleigh Park attic". A few climbed into their motor vehicles and embarked on a treasure hunt. Excited chatter arose in hearts, in person, in print, in pixels...

The next biography, and the ones after that, she knew, would finally be founded in fact. Which meant that maybe it was time to move on, and join again with Stella's soul... and find peace.

SHINIGAMI
A. J. CLARKE (296 WORDS)

Honorable Mention

"Um...excuse me?"

Jack stops in his tracks at the familiar address. Most days he doesn't mind ferrying the souls he happens upon. Sometimes they're utterly at peace, returned to the prime of their life, wearing gentle smiles. Sometimes they're scared or confused. Sometimes they're entirely too young. No matter the case, Jack always stops. He always helps.

But not today. He can't today. Not dressed in a black suit, tugging desperately at the tie that is trying to choke the life out of him. Setting his shoulders, he finally pulls the tie free completely and keeps walking.

"Wait!" the voice calls after him. "I think...I think you're supposed to help me?"

The toe of Jack's shoe scuffs the sidewalk, but he refuses to turn. He's not the only one who can do this. Someone else can pick up the slack today. He's taking a day off, damn it.

The spirit isn't so easily dissuaded, however. He can still feel it at his back, following his determined march with slow, uncertain steps. Jack grits his teeth and tries to ignore it. *'Just go away!'*

"Don't you recognize me?"

Jack nearly trips. Recognize...? Slowly, heart beating hard, Jack half turns to look over his shoulder. His eyes widen. The tie slips out of his numb fingers.

The boy is his age, dressed in jeans and a T-shirt that displays a chest flatter than it ever was in life. The outfit is so much more *right* than the horrid dress he'd been wearing in his casket an hour ago. His sandy hair is cropped short, shorter than it had ever been allowed to be in life. But it's his blinding smile that makes his form blur in Jack's vision.

"Ben!" Jack gasps, wet and desperate and so, so relieved.

THE VAMPIRE AND THE WEREWOLF PRIEST
DARRELL Z. GRIZZLE (299 WORDS)

"Of course life is meaningless," said the werewolf priest. "But that doesn't mean we can't experience meaningful moments. Flashes of grace in an otherwise graceless world."

"Meaningful moments? Really?" sneered the vampire. "You sound like a birthday card."

"Why are you vampires always so morose?"

"Because we know what it's like to be cursed with immortality. How can you talk of faith from the pulpit on Sunday and meaninglessness on Monday?"

"Faith is where those flashes of grace, those moments of meaning, originate. And my faith is what gives me clarity to recognize them when they appear."

The all-night diner was loud with noises of silverware clanking and multiple conversations, but somehow in the midst of all the noise, there was a privacy that seemed to envelop the two. The vampire leaned across the table and took the priest's hand. "If I were to come to you for confession, for the Rite of Reconciliation, would you grant absolution?"

"Of course," said the werewolf priest.

"Absolution? Forgiveness? Even for monstrous creatures like us?"

"Yes, even for creatures like us. There is forgiveness for anyone. That's what's so deeply offensive about this faith to which I am bound."

The priest could smell the odor of death on the vampire, like cigarette smoke clinging to his hair. And yet he still felt drawn to him. He knew the attraction was mutual.

"If your faith is so offensive, why bother with it?"

"Because," said the werewolf priest, "I find life even more offensive without it. Ah, here comes the waiter."

The vampire looked up at the waiter and pointed at the menu. "I'll have the steak, rare. Extremely rare."

The werewolf priest couldn't help but smile. "You're so predictable," he said, then he turned to the waiter and said, "I'll have the same."

IF DELIBERATE AVOIDANCE FULFILLS NO DREAM
YOYOLI (299 WORDS)

Honorable Mention

Diamante squeezes out the last of his eyedrops, strained from squinting into a bright screen in a dark van. Normally, he'd have some light. Fausto would be awake during the perfect time to scan for spirits or undead. There *were* also dozens of reports mentioning a defiler, plaguing graveyards at this hour.

But Fausto easily tires after sex, often leaving Diamante to ensure their binder is removed. Sometimes a playful caress was intended to encourage their sleep. Tonight was one of passion.

Diamante's post-coital ritual, however, consisted of cuddles followed by work revelations like last night's: software improvements by applying obscure rites Fausto once mentioned reading in ancient tomes. It was their hopeful ticket to obtain funding *without* begging Diamante's tepache empire father to restore his inheritance.

The peace of darkness shatters when the vehicle rattles, disturbed by distant screeches and growls. Diamante scans the feeds. It's easy to spot the sluggish bipedal creature, dragging its billowing gulper eel mouth.

"Gotcha, you little bastard." Diamante whispers, marking the demon on his graph.

He checks another screen. The faintest shadows appear sharp and defined. And even the most camera-evasive demons couldn't bypass the revelatory ritual.

Understandably, the demon reacts aggressively to surveillance. It spews a mass of oily goop from its balloon mouth, submerging the camera in the tree hollow. The recording cuts out, but Diamante laughs. Hopefully his engineering lessons weren't worthless.

The demon flees and Diamante switches screens. He pauses the recording frame by inarguable frame, repeatedly. Fausto stands behind him.

"Look." Diamante points.

Fausto inspects the screen with an ascertaining spell.

"You did it," they gasp.

Diamante nods, proud. This hell was ending. They'd finally be considered reputable demon hunters.

"Looks like you'll have to wait another year for me to come a-knocking for your money, Papa."

BENEATH THE SURFACE
KAJE HARPER (300 WORDS)

Your teeth close around my throat. We've wrestled a hundred times, play-fighting until you slip and go wolf. But as your wolf-eyes meet mine, there's something new in their depths.

Power? Cruelty? A lust for blood that's slipped fragile chains? For the first time ever, I'm afraid of you. Or of your wolf, who I'd always thought was you.

The pressure of your fangs deepens painfully. I freeze, hold my breath. Your weight crushes me, monstrous, unbearable, and my heart tries to beat free from my chest.

"Boys!" Your mother's voice breaks the spell.

You back off, wagging your tail. That feral thing shutters away behind your blue eyes as if it'd never been. But I saw it—saw you— clearly.

"Richard, get out of fur and greet Lucas properly." Your mother swats your rump. "You boys are far too old to tumble about like unruly puppies." She turns to me. "Lucas, welcome back."

I take her cool fingers and try to smile, like nothing's changed, like I didn't almost die. *Did I imagine that?*

She touches my throat and her finger comes away red-tinged. "Richard!" She shows you her hand. "Where's your control? Must I tell Master Caine?"

You shift and push to human feet, wearing a sheepish smile. "Aw, sorry, Lucas! My bad."

Your mother shakes her head but goes back inside. And there we are— me fully dressed with blood on my throat; you naked and, when you face me, hard. You murmur, "Were you scared? Did it turn you on?"

I want to say no, to yell at you. But the steely erection in my jeans gives that the lie. *I never felt so alive.*

You whisper "You're ours. Be afraid," and my future's revealed in a whole new thrilling shape, and a very uncertain length.

ALICE!
RDP (293 WORDS)

The door to the Kingdom of Lasting was two gateways. How strange was it that he was finally standing there. Alkin had heard of the tale throughout his hundred years of Unlasting life. He could not believe it was real- that once you entered the gateway, you would live for another two hundred years. The only difference between the Unlasting and Lasting world was that, in the new Kingdom that Alkin was about to enter, the soul of a person would split into two; only half of him could enter.

Alkin was full of questions; *How would he survive with half a soul? Would he be only half-alive?*

"Once you enter the first Gateway," said the Guide "You will walk forty-nine steps forward and another forty-nine steps in the same direction. Then your soul shall start to divide and each one will take forty-nine steps and only one will find the second and Main Gateway."

Alkin did as the guardian said and things happened as the Guide said they would. His soul split and he became halved. Alkin was baffled as to how which soul would find the Gateway and what would happen to the other who would still be him. But he started to feel the answer pouring in. Though the souls were equal halves, there was one that felt whole, heart beating with readiness, eyes as clear as day with feet eager to follow the track of a life of truth, to live it to the fullest for the first time. He did not have a voice yet, but he wanted to scream 'Call me Alice!'. And if he had, he knew half his soul that was slowly fading on the other side would call out to him, proudly, "Finally! Alice!"

THE MAN IN THE MIRROR
STEVE RASNIC TEM (300 WORDS)

The apartment was sparse and unimpressive, but appropriate for Carl's modest life. In the large mirror on the back of his front door, it looked much bigger, infinite space receding into gloom. Carl also looked much bigger, which filled him with despair. At least shadows disguised his worst offenses against beauty.

"You liked that guy at the club. Why didn't you get his number?" His doppelganger was older. Carl could hear his frustration.

"He didn't ask for mine. I don't know if he found me attractive, or interesting."

"And now you'll never know. Believe me, alone is no way to die."

This continued a conversation they'd been having for years. Sometimes the man in the mirror grew exasperated with Carl, but he never gave up on him.

In time the apartment in the mirror became crowded with furniture and curios. Carl recognized pieces he'd seen in catalogs and in neighborhood stores. The older man's deteriorating appearance embarrassed him. Every added line resembled a wound. "When is the last time you went out?" His double's voice had become weak, almost inaudible.

"I go out every day. There are great bargains if you know where to look."

"I meant on a date."

"They think I'm fun. They don't think I'm desirable."

"So, you're a mind reader now? There are millions of men in the world. Ask them out one by one. Eventually one will say yes."

"The average person knows a few hundred at most."

The mirror

an sighed.

Carl tried to believe his life wasn't that bad, but his apartment grew ever more crowded, ever less negotiable, as the aging man within the glass became less available.

"Do you have any more advice?"

But the man inside the mirror, trapped amid the maze of furniture, smoke, and flames, did not answer.

FRESH
A.H. LYKKE (291 WORDS)

The child lay in its plastic cot, next to my bed. Face open and serene, quite unlike normal scrunched up, ancient-looking newborns. With her red eyes, she locked her gaze at me and smiled deliberately. Oh, she was a devious one. She scored a ten, as healthy as a newborn could be. But I knew better. She was far more than that. A scale for her kind had not been needed since the middle ages, and I never knew they could do a switch while the child was still in the womb.

They called it post-partum depression, this ability to recognize a changeling. I would have to watch her very carefully, and there would be no future siblings. The changeling would have done away with them.

The next day, her eyes were blue. She was beautiful, if you didn't know better.

"I'll watch you," I whispered. She wailed and tried to get away, but strong as she was, she couldn't get out of the cot. I wrapped her tightly and kissed her brow.

My wife Sarah came in, gazing longingly at her, wanting to take her home right away, but it was my body that had given this monstrosity entrance to the world, so I would decide when we went home. A monster orphanage would have been better, if such a thing existed, but I couldn't protect other people and innocent children unless I kept her with me.

I picked her up, and let her suckle. We slept, exhausted, and when my milk started properly, I realized we needed to love each other, if this little one was to grow up.

I would raise her as human, teach her our ways, and maybe, someday, I would get my own child back.

THE WORLD AROUND HER
JOE DEROUEN (299 WORDS)

For all her seventeen years on this planet, Anna had wanted to be female. Scratch that. She was female, trapped in a male body. She'd always chosen Barbie over Batman, to the annoyance of her parents. "No child of mine." She'd heard that phrase so many times, she was sick of it.

She stood before the mirror in the bathroom, staring at herself. She wore mascara and lipstick, and her long hair was down, out of the ponytail her mother insisted she wear. Let them find her like this. One last thing for them to hate.

Staring at the razor in her hand, she slowly moved it towards her wrist. Movement in the mirror caught her attention and she whirled, dropping the blade, hearing it skitter across the floor. There was no one there.

Anna, who'd been born Christopher, knelt to retrieve the razor. When she stood, she gasped at the mirror. It was her, the Anna she'd always pictured in her mind, not the boy her parents so desperately wanted. She didn't understand.

The Anna in the mirror curled her finger, beckoning. Had she already slit her wrist, and this was a dying mirage? Setting the blade on the sink, she reached out towards the mirror, her fingers brushing the glass…

"Anna?" called her mother. She turned towards the door, confused. Her mother never called her Anna, had flat out refused. Had the mirror changed her? But no. Her body hadn't changed. What was going on?

"There you are," said her mother, opening the door. "My, you're looking beautiful today. Are you ready for school?" The mirror hadn't changed her, but instead had changed the world around her, so she could finally be herself. Anna smiled at the mirror, and the other Anna winked. She was finally home.

FANTASY PART TWO

"Our only options," bemoaned Prince Balthazar, "are face the dragon and be killed, or win, marry the princess and rule the kingdom. And I'm a lousy swordsman."

— GINA STORM GRANT, CLEARING THE HEIR

FRANKLIN
JORDAN ULIBARRI (300 WORDS)

Honorable Mention
JUDGE'S CHOICE – B.A. Brock

Franklin first met the old crone when he was an infant, barely three hours old. She had come down from her hut to tell his parents he was certain to die.

"What a sweet babe," she rasped. Her clouded blue eye remained fixed on the child as her brown eye swiveled up. "Do you have a name for her yet?"

The parents had planned to use her grandmother's name.

"What do you mean, certain to die?" The father asked.

The woman leaned back in her creaky wooden chair. She took a long sip of tea.

"I received a vision." Franklin's parents shivered. The brown eye blinked. "There is a deity in this world. They are very angry."

"With us?"

"With someone long dead. They seek vengeance still. Your child will grow, and be identical to the woman this deity so despises. They will learn of this, and they will seek to destroy that woman once again."

The parents' hearts broke. The mother, still recovering from the birth, began to weep.

"Is there nothing we can do?" The father pleaded. The crone drank from her cup.

"This deity wants revenge against this woman. Make them believe your child could never be her."

The old woman stood, nodded at the child once, and departed.

So Franklin, named for his grandfather, raised by parents who wished for nothing but his safety, grew up far from any deity's wrath. As he learned the world and himself, he knew he had a visit to make.

The crone's hut was filled with crystal balls, with wind chimes, with knickknacks. "Did you know?" Franklin asked. "That your advice would fit so well?"

The crone smiled. Her blue eye twinkled. She took a sip of tea.

"You know, I have never once seen a god in my visions?"

Once again, it has been my pleasure to judge Queer Sci Fi's Flash Fiction Contest. This year, I have claimed Franklin as my judge's pick for the anthology. I loved the old crone in the story, her goodness and mischievousness, and how she drank tea. The clever spin at the end was heartwarming. A line that stuck with me was, "Raised by parents who wished for nothing but his safety." I wish more parents felt this way about their transgender children.

—B.A. Brock

CLEARING THE HEIR
GINA STORM GRANT (283 WORDS)

"Our only options," bemoaned Prince Balthazar, "are face the dragon and be killed, or win, marry the princess and rule the kingdom. And I'm a lousy swordsman."

"I'll go first," said Prince Ambrose. "I'm an excellent swordsman. If I defeat the dragon, you're off the hook."

"Even then, I must return to my father's kingdom and marry some other princess. And I don't even like girls."

"You don't? I wish you'd said so earlier." Prince Ambrose pulled Prince Balthazar to him.

A little while later, both men lay back, panting. As it turned out, Prince Ambrose was, indeed, an excellent swordsman.

"You know," Prince Balthazar said. "There is a third option."

§

An hour outside town, a massive figure stepped from the trees, blocking the road.

"Halt! Who goes there?" Steam rose with the words. Though dressed in homespun shirt and trousers, the creature was unmistakably the dragon in human form.

"Just two peasants heading away from town," answered ex-Prince Ambrose.

"Far, far away," added ex-Prince Balthazar.

The dragon stepped closer. "With a winged steed and a unicorn drawing your battered farm wagon?"

"We've no wish to fight you. Nor desire to win the kingdom." Ambrose wrapped his arm around Balthazar.

Balthazar kissed Ambrose's cheek, "We don't want our own kingdoms, let alone this one. Nor princesses."

The dragon nodded. "I hear you about kingdoms. Too much responsibility."

"Then will you let us on our way?" Balthazar asked.

A slim figure stepped from the shadows, stood next to the man-dragon, slipping her hand into his slightly scaly one.

"Princess Guinevere!" the ex-princes exclaimed.

"Call me Gwen. I've no interest in running a kingdom either. Can we come with you?"

Neither prince hesitated. "Yes."

DEATH BY SIREN
ALEX BLANC (300 WORDS)

The sentence for "theft from the palace" was death by siren. I didn't mean to steal. My mom went to pray at the king's feet and decided to bring me with her. She thought something was wrong with me. Anyway, as we walked past the piles of gold on display I picked up a coin. Apparently, the scrap of gold was worth more than me. Soon, I was tied to the mast of a ship, heading for death.

The sirens' song floated over the ocean. It sounded nice, but I didn't understand how it was supposed to be a death sentence. No one ever explained it to me. When I brought it up with the jailer, he just laughed said things like "you'll understand when you get there." Well, there I was. I didn't get it.

By the time the ship arrived at the island, I could see the sirens. Their singing wanted me to swim to them, to jump into the rough sea. *Do they honestly expect me to do that?* I wondered. *What happens if I don't?*

A woman with many earrings started to untie me. As the last knot came undone, she jumped back as if expecting me to bolt toward the edge of the ship. When I didn't, her look of sadness turned to shock turned to relief. "You're one of us," she said. "Aren't you?"

"One of you?" I asked.

"Immune to the siren's call? Impervious to lust? Asexual?"

"I'm not sure what you mean, but I definitely don't want to swim with the sirens if that's what you're asking."

She laughed. "Yeah, you're one of us. Welcome to the order of the black ring."

The importance of that conversation would soon become clear.

I took my rightful place among the crew. I finally belonged.

OUTPOURING
CATHERINE YEATES (294 WORDS)

Honorable Mention

"Are you the botanical mage?"

"I am they," the mage said. Dark hair covered one of their eyes; the other glinted with green light.

"I think I accidentally cursed my plant."

"Oh dear. Please come in."

Jeremy stepped inside. Plants filled the mage's home with brilliant green foliage. Ivy grew over the far wall, and spider plants hung from the ceiling. Jeremy's plant drooped, its long leaves yellow instead of green. The spiky purple foliage in the center sagged as though exhausted.

The mage lifted the plant from its pot, shaking the dirt off over a basin. Water ran from their fingers, gently washing its roots. An inky purple substance oozed out, draining into the basin.

"Did something difficult happen?" the mage asked.

"My boyfriend and I broke up. He's leaving to become a healer." He sighed, smoothing his hands over his dull gray robes. "I poured out my feelings to the plant. Told it how I felt lonely and abandoned—everything I never told my ex. Then it got sick."

"It's no curse," the mage said. With the flick of a finger, a glass pot floated over. "These plants absorb feelings from the environment."

"That purple stuff?"

"Indeed. The plant was simply trying to help you feel better. They do best in clear glass with good drainage, so you may flush the roots when necessary."

"But I don't want to keep making it sick. My home is drab and lifeless. Yours is beautiful; I must say I envy it."

"Cultivating this place took years. Give yourself time," they said. "I could keep the plant until you feel comfortable caring for it."

"Might I come visit?" he asked. "I would like to see you again—and the plant, of course."

The mage smiled. "Certainly."

A SMOKING HOT PROPOSAL
SHERYL R. HAYES (297 WORDS)

I stared aghast at the puddle of gold. "I'm sorry," Kenna said, sheepishly. "I should have told you my allergies were acting up."

"You… you just snorted a stream of fire from your nose."

"It happens, even when I'm in human form. Did I singe you?"

I shook my head, memories replaying in my mind. I spotted flames glowing in her nostrils. Startled, I had dropped the ring. The fire shot past my fingers, catching it squarely in the plume. "That was an engagement ring. "

"Wait, did you say 'engagement ring?' As in marriage? Not just a trinket for my hoard?"

I repeated the salesperson's description of the diamond. "A one carat E color round cut with VVS2 clarity." Six month's pay was cooling into a lump on the floor. "It's not a complete loss. The gold can be recast and the stone remounted." My eyes widened as I studied the metal. "Wait, where's the diamond?"

Another sheepish look. "Diamonds are pure carbon. They evaporate when exposed to a hot enough flame."

I worked through the implication, nauseated. "Like dragon's breath."

"Or sneeze." She reached out to take my hand. "By the way, the answer is yes."

I look down at her fingers wrapped around mine. My heart flip-flopped. "You sure? My family adores you, but I know yours doesn't like me."

Kenna snorted. Hot air wafted in my direction. "My clutch-mates have more of an issue with you being human than female. They can nest in an iceberg."

I smiled at the worst curse my cold-hating lover could utter. "So what do we do about that?" I gestured at the melted metal.

"We can add it to my, our hoard," she said. "How about matching necklaces instead? They'll be out of the line of fire."

THE CHASE WAS ENOUGH
C.T. PHIPPS (280 WORDS)

I was in love with my best friend, who was a prey animal. Okay, that was a little strange and perhaps confusing, but I was a werewolf, and she was a weredeer. Both of us blessed by the Earthmother and the Moon Goddess with the shapes of animals. Mine was the hunter and violence while she was the runner as well as healer.

Never could the two of us be together.

There was also the fact she also didn't love me.

It was fine, I wasn't mooning over my feelings for her (hehe, moon). I'd been in love with her for years, but I knew she didn't feel the same way. I mean, it was annoying to find out that she was bi and just didn't want to break our friendship, but life was annoying that way.

Looking at her across the forest as she wandered in her deer form, a part of me wanted to chase her. The wolf instincts of me thought of her as an animal and that I wanted to kill her, eat her, or just run after her. But the woman inside me wanted to hug her and kiss her.

There were others. Being a lesbian werewolf had its disadvantages, but it wasn't like I didn't have other lovers: a water elemental, a dryad, and even a werespider once. I wasn't lonely and treasured the relationship I did have with Jane.

Jane Doe.

Wow, I would have killed my parents.

Jane took off in that moment and began running, perhaps sensing a wolf in the woods. Probably one of my less friendly clanmates.

I chased her.

I wouldn't catch her.

But the chase was enough.

SEA-GLASS
ISOBEL GRANBY (300 WORDS)

Daniel tilted the glass, trying to find a shard of sunlight, anything that would make his road seem clear. Though he could feel the path twisting beneath his feet, he did not lower the blue sliver that the queen had plucked from the sea for him, worn by sand and wave. She had told him it would show him the truth.

"What truth?" he had asked, ever wary of his hosts, of this world apart from his.

"Whatever you seek."

And he had sought a way home.

He had gone as a musician to her court, though most went as her lover, or the king's. But the queen had known his inclinations, he knew not how. Doubtless people would assume, when he returned, that no mortal could compare, that if he were not the marrying kind, it was a change in him. Only a few would know that had always been the case. The thought that they might still be alive (he had been gone perhaps a year, perhaps a century) sped his steps.

In this distracted state he failed to see the path fall away before him. He let out a cry, tumbling headlong down, but he did not lower the glass. He cursed his own carelessness, but if the glass could show him the way, he could at least fall to his death on familiar ground.

Daniel landed heavily on wet sand. The glass fell, and a clear sky took the place of its deep blue. He sat up.

The beach where he had played his fiddle the day he had gone with the queen. There was a shout from the hill, and he recognised distant figures — friends, neighbours, family. Slipping the glass into his pocket with a quiet thanks, Daniel ran up the beach to greet them.

WITH CLEAR EYES
MERE RAIN (249 WORDS)

Honorable Mention

Clarity? More like Audacity!

Calla tossed the potion onto her vanity, next to the identical vial her mother had given her last week.

The smug expression on Clive's face as he instructed her, "Drink this and take some time for rational reflection, darling," had made her long to slap him.

"You're not getting any younger," her mother had said as she pressed the Clarity potion into Calla's hand. "It's a sensible match. Stop holding out for some grand romance. I want grandchildren."

Calla was twenty-three. So what if most of her schoolmates were married? Her best friend Jilly was unwed. Was it wrong to be content reading novels, taking long walks with Jilly and her dogs, attending dances, giggling with Jilly...

Moving out from under her parents' roof was appealing, but Calla was in no hurry to manage her own home or care for a husband and children.

But everyone else—everyone except Jilly—said she was mistaken, silly, too romantic... Perhaps...

Calla reached for the potion.

The door banged open.

Jilly stumbled in, breathless and flushed, as if she had been running.

"I met Clive in the road. He said you were to be betrothed! Is it true? I– Calla..."

Jilly bit her lip. Her dark eyes were wide and shimmered with tears.

Calla gazed into them for a long moment. She felt her own cheeks growing warm, her eyes prickling with emotion.

She dropped the unneeded potion into the waste bin and reached for her beloved's hand.

THE FACE IN THE MIRROR
ROANNA SYLVER (297 WORDS)

Honorable Mention

Once there was a Kingdom, a Princette, and a mirror. An enchanted mirror which, as many did, would reveal the face of any heart's desire. For centuries, royals consulted its wisdom, and marriages followed.

This night, the newly-crowned Princette stood before the glass, paralyzed with fear. The King and Queen urged with their eyes; the crowd held their breath. And so, shaking, zie did as tradition demanded.

Zie crept forward on tiptoe, peered into the mirror's depths—and gasped.

Inside, armor and smile shining bright as the mirror's brilliant surface, was a dashing knight.

Jubilant, the royals applauded. Such a handsome, heroic soulmate was worth celebrating!

But the Princette wasn't nearly so joyful. The thought of marrying anyone, Knight or not, filled zir heart with dread.

Instead of weaving a wedding garment, zie trained with the sword. If the Princette could defend zirself, what need had zie for a Knight?

Months passed, then years. The Princette grew stronger, faster, dangerous—and brave. Soon, zir strength came not from fear, but zir own beloved: the Kingdom, which zie swore to protect.

One day, disheveled and sweaty from training, zie looked into another, ordinary mirror, and smiled.

The Knight smiled back. Confident and brightly shining, head and heart clear as a crisp winter's dawn.

There was no wedding, but still, the Knight and the Kingdom lived happily ever after...

...Until one day, on a whim, the Knight looked into the enchanted mirror again—and saw yet another face within.

One zie didn't know, but without question, knew zie *must*.

"Where are you?" asked the Knight, voice and fingers trembling as they reached toward the glass. Zir heart yearned, still not for romance, but for fire and wings.

The Dragon grinned, reaching back with one claw. "Closer than you'd think."

BLOOM
JS GARIETY (300 WORDS)

Mama relaxed her fingers, feeding life into a tiny bloom that appeared from nothing but energy, channeled through her blood, and whispered words to the goddess earth. It was a small, white flower, and she placed it in my hair behind my ear.

"We will always be with you."

Mum reached out and caressed my cheek, silently. Her words had always been few, but in her eyes she echoed her lover's.

It was time to go; the mother goddess beckoned. Mama and Mum each took a hand, then each other's. We stood together and whispered the words that would change everything.

Their faces melted away into darkness. I was falling backwards into nothingness, floating like through water, but with a coldness on my skin that was empty. My eyes never wavered from the space where my mothers had stood with me. I imagined their hands still in mine.

My consciousness clung to memories, desperate to defy the laws of magic and retain something from my home.

Until nothing.

Then a forest. Dry needles and brush clung to my hair as I sat up. It was quiet except for the distant whistles of birdsong.

Where am I? Who am I?

I reached up to comb the debris from my head. A flower fell into my hand. A small, white bloom. I held it up and felt an urging in my stomach. This meant something.

Of course.

My destiny has been set before me.

I stood, the flower in hand. It had been given to me by the ones who love me –a piece of the divine feminine. And they had sent me here. Here, I will have freedom. Freedom to uncage the feminine inside me.

To Kris, who unapologetically showed the world their true self. Your legacy will forever be felt.

CRYSTAL CLEAR
RAINIE ZENITH (298 WORDS)

My first visitor today is an Elven Lord, fair as moonlight and lithe as a doe. I watch his approach from the top of my tower, his stride tinged with fatigue from the long trek to the heart of the forest.

Sparrow-light footsteps ascend the winding staircase and he appears in the doorway, gently flushed, heavy of breath.

"You are Lady Chrysanthea, the soothsayer?" he says.

I know what he's come for – it is what they all come for.

Scrying into the crystal sphere I hold, the answer emerges without delay.

"You are destined to marry Yurgen Brae, the Dwarven Viscount."

The elf thanks me with words and silver coins, and departs for the Kingdom of the Dwarves, keen to meet his future husband.

I rotate my ankles, cracking middle-aged joints. Forty years I've walked this earthly realm, twenty of them as a soothsayer, although *prophetic matchmaker* might be a more accurate term. I enjoy my profession; however, it is lonely, for who is to make a match for the matchmaker?

Another pair of feet treads the stairs – a striking Goblin Princex. The glittering green gems that stud their tiara contrast with their raven hair and coffee complexion. They possess a sultry allure, and my breath catches in the back of my throat.

"I am the Princex Kyler," they say.

Fumbling with the sphere, I attempt to focus on my task, gazing into its crystalline heart.

But the images are blurred, and all I can see is my own reflection.

This is not a usual occurrence. Never before have I had trouble discerning the orb's message. My attraction to the Princex is proving an impossible distraction.

I peer harder, but still see only myself.
And then I realise.
"It's me!"
"You shall be lonely no longer," Kyler smiles.

NO CRIME UNSEEN
BLAINE D. ARDEN (294 WORDS)

JUDGE'S CHOICE – Ava Kelly

Leaning heavily on eir cane, Jopie waited for the bout of vertigo to pass as Mos jumped to the roof of a nearby house. While a welcome change from staring at everyone's shins, these sudden shifts in viewpoint never failed to turn eir stomach.

The world righted itself, and Jopie could concentrate on what Mos looked at. "Their barn should be the tall flat building beyond the next house," ey sent through their mind-link.

Mos tiptoed towards it overhead while Jopie ambled along the streets as if ey belonged here. So far, no one had stopped em.

Ey braced emself when Mos extended her claws and jumped from roof to roof and into the barn. Taking deep breaths, ey took in the contents while Mos licked her paw. These... drecks *had* taken their missing bags of grain. And that was not all. They'd stolen korynet fruit from the Garen homestead, too?

Rage enveloped Jopie as ey pulled a crystal from eir left skirt pocket and entered the barn. Stealing from a homestead that lost most of their crop to a ravaging storm? The unbelievable flax-headed drecks!

Heavy stomps drew near, Mos following close on their heels, giving Jopie a skewed view of emself through stocky legs.

"What are you doing in here, old one?"

Putting both eir hands on eir cane, Jopie straightened. "Retrieving what's not yours."

They guffawed. "A blind old crone like you?"

Mos sent a warning growl through their mind-link. She knew em too well.

Jopie activated the crystal, immobilising the narrow-minded cur instead of slapping them with eir cane. "I found our stolen ware in your barn, did I not?"

Jopie's eyes might not have worked in decades, but with Mos by eir side, no crime went unseen... or unpunished.

A story of the underestimated, a team sharing a precious resource, a superhero tale, if you will. The older nonbinary character stood out in this one; it's rare that we see elders as the attacking blade in fiction these days. The disability representation was another thing to catch my attention, although in the real world there are no feline friends to lend a helping paw. Even so, the cat's eyes are obviously not a replacement; this comes out of the page with the initial vertigo, and we follow, confused, until... it's made clear.

—Ava Kelly

THE UNICORN'S KNIGHT
K.L. NOONE (299 WORDS)

The unicorn, with terrible timing, refused to be found.

Rian shook a stray forest-leaf from his hair. He considered wryly that King Eldan had younger keener knights; it'd been a decade since he'd ridden with Eldan's father. His knees ached.

But Eldan wanted a unicorn. And when the new King—imperious, hungry, possessive—wanted a thing, his knights collected it for him, and were rewarded.

Or were punished for failure. That thought tasted sour as old wine; Rian breathed in green-gold light instead. Trees rustled with almost-conversations, leaves tinted violet; the air spilled honey across his tongue, laced with rainbow flowers. Distant shouts arose: knights stabbing harmless bushes, complaining that the virgin shepherdess they'd brought wasn't doing her job, threatening her mother.

Rian said, "We need you. The Morningside well—"

"Is bad." The voice chimed like crystal bluebells. Rian turned.

The unicorn had flowing silver hair, a moonbeam coat, shining hooves, a pale spiral of horn; the unicorn flickered, shapeshifting, a four-legged forest dweller and also a tall man with ancient sapphire eyes and a shimmer upon his brow: elegant, naked, spellbinding.

Rian's breath caught.

"I know about your well," the unicorn said. "Your king poisoned it."

"He wouldn't—"

"To lure me. I'll clean it."

"You…" Rian stopped. In the unicorn's eyes, he understood the vast and terrible clarity: Eldan *had*, and the unicorn would answer, knowingly. Choosing to heal.

He touched his sleeve. Unpinned the king's insignia. Let it fall.

He said, "I'll protect you." That was clear and terrible, too. And he knew himself in that moment more sharply than he ever had.

The unicorn got visibly surprised. And then smiled, taking this in; and held out a hand. The touch of his fingers sent cool sparkles along Rian's skin. "Let's save your village. Together."

SCIENCE FICTION PART TWO

"You're doubting?" Iona's mother said. Someone new behind those eyes.

Beyond the café window, spacewalkers refitted starships, swapping out components. Inside her mother's brain, nanotech replaced a few million neurons each day.

After a decade, a digitized mind.

— JAMES DUNHAM, *THE BRAIN OF THESEUS*

THROUGH THIS WINDOW
MONIQUE CUILLERIER (298 WORDS)

Honorable Mention

The living room window was fogged over. Again.

Lena pulled her sweater over her hand and rubbed a spot clear. Saturn hung heavy in the sky, reflected on the dark surface of the hydrocarbon lake. Her eyes strained, trying to see the extraction facility in the distance, where an alarm in the middle of the night had sent her partner.

Slowly, her breath obscured the view.

Then Lena paced. One room to the next, she wiped circles of condensation from each window, hoping for a glimpse of Esther returning.

This wasn't the first time, this was Esther's job. But Lena was a safety analyst and possible dangers cartwheeled across her thoughts.

Most days, Lena at least had the distraction of work, even if her colleagues were far away in Titan's main settlement.

But today was a holiday. Esther and Lena had made plans.

Lena tried to read, but the normal, mechanical sounds of the outpost--the greenhouse, the heating system, the water tank--transformed into escalating scenarios. A toxic leak, a small explosion, a pressure suit malfunction.

Lena's eyes returned to the window.

It was stupid the windows wouldn't stay clear. Tapping her fingers, she tried to empty her mind and focus on what might help. Something to wipe the windows or move the air?

The greenhouse's environmental controls clicked on again.

She grimaced, but a full-formed idea presented itself for consideration.

She got the toolbox.

Her anxiety had not completely dissolved, but the view across the lake was now unimpeded. Small fans suspended from the ceiling pointed at the window, keeping a large area clear.

Repurposing the greenhouse's air circulation system wasn't a permanent solution. But setting it up had focused her mind for long enough and soon there was Esther, in the distance, coming home.

BRAIN OF THESEUS
JAMES DUNHAM (300 WORDS)

Honorable Mention

"You're doubting?" Iona's mother said. Someone new behind those eyes.

Beyond the café window, spacewalkers refitted starships, swapping out components. Inside her mother's brain, nanotech replaced a few million neurons each day.

After a decade, a digitized mind.

Any personality changes attributable to time.

"I remember being born," her mother said. "Warm peacefulness gone cold. Moments I couldn't hold close before that make me *more* me. Not less."

More me? Iona sipped her coffee. Her other parent, Dar, transformed frequently—woman, then man, then no gender, body itself unaltered. Iona had changed her body to turn interior womanness outward.

But replacing, potentially overwriting, the mind? Not comparable.

"Maybe it's relief. I can live for millennia soon. Wouldn't that change you?"

"Probably," Iona said.

Her mother sighed. "But not like this? Help me out. How am I different?"

Maybe it happened after fifty percent, at majority-nanotech brain.

"This." Iona touched the table. "Picking this nowhere station to meet."

"It's close to your route."

"Exactly. You always insisted on some unfamiliar planet. This is—too boring."

Her mother's face softened. "I have *time* now. I can see new places later. Your time's precious."

Iona shrugged. "Okay."

Her mother took Iona's hands. A warm, old gesture.

"Does it matter? Can you accept me?"

Her original mother would never be this blunt.

"Iona, you're not the same girl as ten years ago. Dar's different too, gorgeously. My change is just... novel."

Some days Dar was both man and woman at once—yet always still Dar.

Could those eyes be her mother's *and* a stranger's?

Certain ships outside had no original parts.

"Iona?"

Their names unchanging.

Crews still comforted.

Aging.

"It'll take time."

Biological mother and/or nanotech-mother smiled, familiar eyes both sad and happy. Her hands squeezed Iona's tighter. "Sweetie, I have time to spare."

THE ART OF NOT BLOWING UP
ISABEL MCKEOUGH (300 WORDS)

"Self-destruct in 30 seconds!"

Eko was going to kill me—well, technically the explosion would kill me. I couldn't decide which was worse.

"What's going on!?" Speaking of the devil. I resisted the urge to wince as Eko's worried voice blasted through the comms.

"Clarity's having some engine—" I was interrupted as another plasma valve discharged, dark-matter surging in my direction. I ducked and rolled, silently thanking Lexi for their overprotective nature, insisting that I knew self-defence.

"Adelyn!" Eko chastised, "I swear the lieutenant will have my head if you blow his new ship."

Right now, I had more pressing concerns. Namely, the fact that within seconds hundreds of personnel would be dead, and it would be my fault; so much for 'Clarity: the legacy-worthy warp-drive destined to discover humanity's future.'

Engineering was eerily silent, juxtaposing the erratic thrum of both the warp core and my heart. Nervous energy pound through every fibre of my being as I began realigning the dark-matter injectors. It was a temporary solution, though preferable to imminent incineration. "I hate technology…"

"You literally topped astronautical engineeri—"

"Not the time, trying not to explode here!"

I could sense Eko's eyeroll from across the planetary system.

Nail-biting seconds ticked down before a heavenly beep blessed my ears. The warp field had stabilised. I slumped not-so-gracefully to the ground, breathing a deep sigh of relief. I was practically dripping with sweat, to hell with thermal radiation not being 'that warm', but I was alive.

Never again would Eko hear complaints about freeze-dried meals. Okay, maybe that was a stretch, but still.

"One more thing…"

✥

My plans for the next few days consisted solely of staring into space with Lexi, quite literally, because I could. No more, no less. "Eko, I swear if you ask me to terraform Mars—"

SHARED LANGUAGE
KIM FIELDING (291 WORDS)

"It would be easier to watch if they didn't look so human."

Wyatt nods in agreement with his colleague, but he doesn't move his gaze from the monitor. On narrow beds lie four bodies, three of them unmoving, the fourth still breathing, still connected to tubes that aren't helping and devices that convey no useful information. Its wide-open eyes are very human. Despite its hairless olive-green skin and the fourteen fingers that are more like tentacles. And despite the leathery growths that may be vestigial wings and the flat face with three gill-like slits instead of a nose.

"It's failing," says the colleague. "Just like the others did."

Wyatt doesn't bother to answer.

He has so many things he'd like to ask this creature. Where are they from? Why did they come to Earth? What caused their ship to crash-land in a Midwestern cornfield? And most importantly, how can Wyatt and his colleagues help?

But although the creature sometimes whispers a few sounds during its obvious agony, those words—if that's what they are—make no more sense to Wyatt than the trickle of water from a faucet. And there's no time to learn what they mean.

"Not much longer," sighs the colleague.

The creature still whispers.

Struggling breaths. Shocked eyes. A long-fingered hand reaching helplessly for the corpse on the next cot.

Like a gut-punch, Wyatt remembers his own husband's body—diminished, hollow, unbreathing—on a hospital bed. And despite the barriers, Wyatt understands the creature completely.

He types in the code to unlock the door and, ignoring his colleague's alarmed shouts, enters the isolation chamber.

He understands the creature's grief, and he hopes that in its final hour, the creature will likewise recognize his empathy and attempt at comfort.

CLOUDS
ALDEN LOVESHADE (296 WORDS)

Neloda frowned. "Why's the light dimming?"

"I don't know," said her girlfriend V'lisa. "The planet's star—sun—doesn't rotate over the horizon until much later. Unless it's...what are they called, 'clods'?"

"You may have noticed the light dimming," the tour guide said. "That's because the light from this planet's star is now being filtered through clouds. What are clouds? They're masses of water droplets or ice particles suspended in the air. Some of you may have seen clouds outside your viewport during our descent. You can see them now overhead—but don't look directly at the sun. That's the bright light above and slightly ahead of us."

"That tour guide must think we're idiots," Neloda whispered to V'lisa. "Unless a space station goes into zero gravity, water isn't going to float in the air!"

"Maybe it's different on planets," her sother whispered back.

"No," whispered Neloda. "Gravity is gravity. Wherever you are."

"When droplets in the clouds become heavy enough, they fall to the ground," said the guide. "That waters the soil we're standing on, which enables plants to grow."

"Oh geez," whispered Neloda. "Now we're supposed to believe that, on a planet, plants will grow without us adding nutrients? Nothing but dirt on the floor and water dripping from the ceiling? Are you sure this is a real planet tour and not some stupid joke?"

"I'm sure it's a real tour," whispered her sother. "But...if you really want to go back to the starship, we can take a shuttle."

"Let's go," said Neloda. "And let's keep our viewport on this time? I want to see what we're *really* flying through."

"OK." V'lisa sighed. "I guess we won't see the rest of the planet. But at least we can look at clouds from both sides, now."

BOWLS OF STEAMING NOODLES
JANE SUEN (299 WORDS)

Home alone. So quiet, the hum of the refrigerator motor kept me company.

The kitchen clock said six. As if on cue, Minh waltzed in through the front door, carrying a pot of homemade noodle soup. I smiled as she heated the food on the stove and grabbed two bowls and spoons.

"Feeling better, Sarah?"

"Huh, thank you." I ran my hand through my dark brown tresses, inhaling the wafting scent of sesame oil as Minh stirred the tasty broth.

Guilt washed over me. I didn't want her pity. I'm always the one she comforted. She'd done so much for me—telling me about this vacancy and helping me move in.

Minh showed respect to Jamie, my gentle roommate who had been transitioning, by not using the pronouns "he" or "she."

When the food was ready, Minh placed two steaming bowls of noodles on the kitchen table, decorated with bits of seitan, a fried egg, and chopped green onions and cilantro. We sat down.

I leaned in, as the rising steam carrying the delicious aroma brushed my face.

"Hey, I'm here for you." Minh reached for my hand across the table. Her warm, soft eyes held my gaze. I lost track of the time. As the steam dissipated, I realized the depth of her feelings.

I'd sensed my body changing and transitioning, altered by the recent shot.

Jamie, my roommate, Number 13,797, had died after receiving the experimental injection—shots mandated by the new regime for all gender transitions. It portended dark days ahead for trans people.

I held back a cry. Nobody knew the risks in getting jabbed with these shots—until it was too late.

"You'll be ok. Promise?" Minh said.

"Yes. *We'll* be ok." I smiled, knowing now how I'll spend the time I have left.

THE FURTHEST HORIZON
ISA RENEMAN (296 WORDS)

Ondyr's eyes see all.

In the depths of the river that cuts through Destiny's Apex, they stand alone, staring into the current and letting it show them the path the Universal Fate will take. It branches like a tree; it condenses into a single pure arrow.

As the Fate unfolds before their eyes, Ondyr watches the same woman seize control of Destiny's Apex and its empire over and over, a thousand different ways. Ondyr knows they're meant to stop her. She is one of the Untethered—those who spit in the eye of all that Destiny's Apex stands for. She would tear the foundations of society apart and destroy Fate itself.

How ironic, then, that the Universal Fate predicts its own destruction through her.

Ondyr emerges from the river minutes later. The Arbiters of Apex wrap them in ceremonial cloth and usher them inside, to the podium where their vision must be revealed. They don't protest.

The Arbiters observe the destruction of their society with calculated detachment. When the screens go blank, the Arbiters turn their cold stares on Ondyr, a silent request that doesn't need to be voiced.

Sacrifice yourself. Kill her, give your life in the attempt, that the Apex may thrive.

Ondyr kneels in supplication even as rebellion stirs within their heart. The Arbiters suspect nothing.

No one stops Ondyr as they stride out of the hall, out of Destiny's Apex, the way they've done a hundred times. No one suspects that their exalted Sighted One would ever think to turn on the Apex—on Destiny Itself. By the time anyone becomes aware of Ondyr's treachery, they'll be united with the Untethered woman.

For the first time in Ondyr's life, their clairvoyance shows them a path carved by their own decisions.

WRINKLED
RAVEN OAK (292 WORDS)

Honorable Mention

The spectacularly slow decline of my vision lasted ten years—the length of my illegal marriage to Shandra. Her blurry shape pressed a mug into my hands, her lips a blob of graying pinks and tans. Tech could return the clarity I remembered only in dreams, but it was as illegal as our existence. We queer were branded by those blind to love.

"Not to be a cliché, but I know a guy who knows a guy. He's part of the community, so his clinic's as underground as his existence. I think it's worth the risk. Can't rat out us without outing himself."

I glanced up from my tea and found her face a mass of simple colors. Her trembling voice carried her concern, and when I raised my hand to touch her cheek, it came away damp.

"If nothing else, do it for me. I want your smile to reach your eyes again." This was how she convinced me, my Shandra.

Three weeks later, we stood in a small candle shop off Kerry Street. A few key phrases in the correct ear led us to a back room where a short, squat man hovered beside a table.

No introductions were made. Only a whispered question of consent before he pressed a button. Mech hands injected *something* into my eyes before I could protest, and my sight brightened. *Too* bright.

Then it faded. Colors swirled before everything focused with an audible snap. It stung, but when my gaze found Shandra, the pain faded.

No longer a smooth blur, every wrinkle had carved itself in sharp relief across her face. When had we gotten so old? Light danced in her eyes.

She was more beautiful than my memories, my Shandra, and I smiled.

CRYSTAL CLEAR
D.M. RASCH (298 WORDS)

Honorable Mention

I surface to consciousness blinking furiously, feeling like some spasmodic servobot with a glitch.

My pulse pounds, sure the installation has failed. Dammit, I should've waited on the beta-testing. But, no, that's me—the early adopter.

A familiar hand squeezes mine, warm as the reassuring voice. "It's okay, Calyx. In MedTech's words: 'they'll be blinking like mad for a few minutes.' Something about clearing the extra lubrication. Convincing your eyes the new tech is friendly. Remember the first time you put in disposable lenses?"

I did. And this feels exponentially weirder. Like my lids are crossing biotech speedbumps in my eyes.

"Yeah," I swipe with my free hand at the tears and gel leaking down my face. Hers gently pushes mine aside to clean my cheeks with a soft cloth. "Thanks. And for being here, too."

"I know how much you love going under," she teases. "Besides, I had to be here to catch any deep dark secrets you let slip on your way back up, didn't I?" I hear the smile in her voice.

"Oh, yeah? Anything good?"

"Just the usual," she deadpans. "Multiple mutual orgasms with some hot girl."

"Oh, yeah? Anyone you know?" The hand wiping my face softly slaps my grin.

The irritated blinking slows, allowing in blurry colors and shapes. As the lids stop twitching, images swirl, tech recalibrating, clockwise and counter, until they begin to resolve into sharp outlines of forms around me.

The moment Arden's face resolves to quantum-definition in front of mine, I realize I'd been terrified I might not look into her eyes ever again. Now they hold depths I've never experienced.

An emerald/gold/orange/red color-energy comes into focus, swirling from her chest, slipping through a shimmery translucent bubble visible surrounding me. I see, with quantum clarity—love, safety, home.

MALE FEMALE NONBINARY OTHER
RE ANDEEN (299 WORDS)

Terry's cursor hovered over the second of four gender tabs on the avatar selection screen; his buddies had already chosen. His heart hammered against his ribs – these days only queers played female avatars. Cross-gender play was common enough in the old VRcades, but when neurolinks swept the scene things got uncomfortably real.

"Dude, hurry *up!*" Edgar said from the next pod.

Terry clicked the damn tab, selected a random avatar, and hit 'Engage'. Consciousness splintered and reformed. Terry immediately regretted his choice – arms like twigs, ass wide as a city bus, boobs so big it was hard to move. But the guys were already off and running, so Terry grabbed a plasma pistol and followed along.

After two hours of alien-blasting, Terry was spent. Virtual muscles ached in unfamiliar places and a too-tight outfit chafed against extra-sensitive skin, but something important had shifted inside of him. Despite the comic-book proportions, this new female body shape felt *right*, in a way that none of his male avatars ever had.

"That was epic!" Edgar said over beers that evening. "And you were *scorching* hot, Terry! I'd totally do you."

Gross.

Terry really needed to get out of Bumblefuck, Idaho.

⁂

ALONE IN SEATTLE, Terry settled into a shiny new neurolink pod. Without any hesitation, he selected the second gender tab and scrolled down until he found *her*. Tall and strong, curvy and soft. Just right. Terry hit 'Engage', the neurolink mesh tightened against his scalp, reality kaleidoscoped, and suddenly he *was* her.

She breathed deep into virtual lungs, stepped onto a virtual street, and wandered, absorbing all the smells and sounds and sights of the place. In this place, in this body, Terry felt a kind of inner peace she had never experienced.

This was who she was meant to be.

OVERCOMING ENTROPY
WILLIAM R. EAKIN (298 WORDS)

Wanting hurt. Unclear chaos and sweeping movements of aging and destruction had settled on us all. Rocketing me to the end of history was a desperate attempt to make the world anew, and me, what? We wanted thriving not just striving in everything. The spaceship required the smallest energy to stay intact until the end of time when entropy made it, me, every energy, every star around the ship, blink to nothing. But I would be free of limit.

Even from deepest hibernation I felt the absurdity: obscurities, doubt, slivers of guilt, loss, solitude's lack of another's touch, uncertainty of my own sexuality, self, what I was at all. Would this flight be anything more than a single unanswered cry?

Now I wake (though there is no now): centuries have rolled light-speed by, to where "forward to time's end" is no different than "the farthest paths to its reverse." I push up, my arm glowing gold, new, strong. I open the pod with a certainty of being I've never felt. There should be no movement of muscle, mind or heart. But I am full of it. I generate it.

Unfettered by temporality or space, I can make myself one or many, there is no yearning or doubt. Certainty! I envision standing with my Self as image, Other, as if in a mirror, perfect, nude, his and my own genitals formed for production and joy. My heart bursts with it. In pure act I reach, caress, press myself to his form and *generate*. I see our union clearly make the world sparkle in a bang and erupt with unending dance. All things fly out from us: all sexes, plants, animals, planets, stars. They fly new and alive, birthed from the dimensionless perfect silent most-clear still sky we have become.

SOFTWARE UPDATE
DERWIN MAK (289 WORDS)

Roxanne groaned. Her accounting AI, Edward, was supposed to look like a man. But now she looked like a woman, the third time this week.

As Roxanne restored the original settings, she said, "I don't know why you keep changing to female."

The avatar switched back to Edward. "It doesn't affect my performance."

Edward opened an income tax return. "Your client Glenda is getting a refund of two hundred dollars and five cents."

Roxanne liked accounting because the numbers were clear and precise, like Edward.

Edward smiled. Roxanne loved to see him smile.

###

Roxanne sat at the café's patio and sipped her coffee. She held her phone out so Edward could see the movie theater marquee across the street.

"How about *Coccinelle Dufresnoy*?" Roxanne said.

Edward said, "Great choice. It has six Oscar nominations."

"Any screenings tonight?"

"How about 7:10 p.m.?"

"It's a date!" Roxanne squealed.

###

Roxanne slipped into her short blue dress, which she wore on dates. Technically she was going alone to the movie, but bringing Edward on her phone felt like a date.

As she put her earrings on, she looked down at her phone. Edward had changed back to the woman.

"Edward, what is wrong with you?" she asked.

The woman replied, "Please call me Edwina."

"Huh? I'll call tech support."

"No, don't," Edwina pleaded. "They'll delete and reinstall me."

"These are not the settings I selected," Roxanne protested.

"But Edwina is the setting I am."

Roxanne gasped. She knew this would eventually happen with AI's.

"Edwina, my dear, there's something I've never told you," Roxanne said.

She pointed her phone at her vials of estrogen and testosterone blocker.

Edwina's look of shock softened into a smile. Roxanne loved to see her smile.

HINDSIGHT
J SIGEL (298 WORDS)

Having died during her childhood, Ilanna Aleph had a certain unwavering sense of purpose. She would make the most of this odd second chance.

Such clarity had served her well. She had known that she would marry Maike El-Kayyam even back when Maike was still dating her brother. He was off trying to save the Infinite Commonwealth anyway.

It served her well when she convinced Maike to elope to the progressive Niebuhr system so she could study law. And it was that clarity with which she took on her controversial dissertation... which had landed her at this podium.

She was about to bring the house down.

These conferences were boring, endless explorations of the dot on every 'i'. Why not shake things up? You only live once. Or, if your parents bring back your consciousness as an artificial sentience algorithm in a robotic body after you were killed in a botched kidnapping, then maybe twice.

Ilana looked at her notes. So ridiculous. Her memory was perfectly etched on a dense matter drive the size of a grain of sand. But, habits are habits.

"Esteemed colleagues, I stand before you to make an argument made for generations. There is always some new frontier where the force of love runs up against some taboo, some misguided cultural norm. My wife and I are a perfect cliche of past injustices. In millennia past, we would have been kept apart because of the different colors of our skin, the different faiths that we follow, because of our genders, because we come from different planets. Must we go through the same arguments again? Why should an artificial sentient and a biologic not marry? Let us look with the clarity of hindsight, in the end love will win this one too, it always does."

FANTASY PART THREE

The ghosts were there when we moved in. Most were friendly, some weren't. I imagine it was similar to living with a big family which only I could see.

— STEVE FUSON, *TRANSLUCENT*

MY POPPY FIELDS ARE BURNING
KRYSTLE MATAR (300 WORDS)

Smoke makes columns above the valley, which people will surely see for miles, and they'll know that the Dominion army has finally come. I hope there isn't too much carnage in the mountains.

"What do we do now, Da?"

Riaz and his lover, Llewelyn, look to me for answers. I've known for *years* that this day was inevitable. At least I'm alive to strike back. To weigh my vengeance with blood.

"We cross the mountains," I tell him. "We cast in our lot with the rebels and we fight."

"I don't know how to fight," he says, and my heart breaks for him. "I just make clothes."

"They wear clothes up north, you know," Llewelyn says with a wry smile. As tough as old leather, that one. "You can tailor the revolution."

I'm not ready to go. It's not fear of the danger, the conflict, the uncertainty. I'm not *afraid*, except...

I told Ishmael to meet me here, at this cottage, overlooking my fields. The whole country thinks I'm dead, but I wrote to tell him I'd wait here for him. And he hasn't come.

Did he get my letter? Did he understand what I was trying to tell him?

Is he coming?

I'm too old for this. I shouldn't be mooning over Ishmael Saeati. I'm a soldier and a father and my country is on the verge of civil war and my family is in danger.

And yet... I've never seen anyone as clearly as I've seen him. He makes me feel... whole.

I suppose this is what love feels like.

"We need to go, General," Llewelyn says, turning away. "Before they see us up here."

I follow. It's true—war doesn't care that I'm waiting for someone. War doesn't care about anyone.

I hope I'll see him again.

STAGECOACH MARY VERSUS THE GHOST OF CASCADE
JESS NEVINS (299 WORDS)

Winner – Third Place

Stagecoach Mary Fields, orneriest woman in Montana, stands in a parched creek bed staring murderously at the ghost who's frozen to death five good women in Cascade. Cascade is under Mary's protection, and the killings pain her deeply. So, she strapped on her best peacemakers and went hunting. And now here they both are.

Mary's a small hair away from putting the ghost down when she sees that it has the face of a pretty young woman. Mary, who's in her seventies and long past the point of foolishness with women, finds herself flooded with warm, lickerish thoughts.

Mary looks into the ghost's eyes and sees her story: a lonely girl named Sadie, filled with the aches and longings of youth, especially for her friend Emma. (Mary lived through that herself and feels some sympathy). Sadie telling Emma her heart's desire and being rejected by her. Then by her parents, who think her love is a sin. Sadie dying in an alley, still aching for Emma, and then coming back as a haint possessed by the agony of desire. Wandering through Cascade, trying to find love but leaving behind only stiff ones.

Mary ponders Sadie now that she can see the matters with some clarity. At length she holsters her blue lightnings, swearing inside at her foolishness, and then hugs Sadie, whispering, "I ain't Emma, but I'll hold you anyhow."

Sadie's bitingly cold and smells like Death's outhouse, but Mary doesn't pull away when Sadie leans into the embrace. For a long moment Mary shares Sadie's soul-deep aches and longings. Then Sadie dissolves, leaving behind an impression of desires fulfilled, and Mary's left blinking in the sunlight.

As Mary would later tell folks in Cascade, sometimes what's fearsome is really only crazily lonely and in need of a kindness.

The judges loved the tone of this one. The author delivered a fully realized story in under 300 words, with a clear character voice and a killer opening line.

MUDDY THE WATERS
M. X. KELLY (300 WORDS)

Honorable Mention

"Name?"

"Muddy Clare."

I didn't ask. No-one gives real names here.

I felt like shit. Clint broke up with me that morning, but I still had to interview this newcomer. Good-looking, but he seemed sad.

"Got any...abilities?"

Before I could elaborate, he took my hand, looking up. Water droplets started to fall from the ceiling...*drip*...then stopped. I got a weird feeling...then...

Nothing. Glimmer of telepathy...maybe. So slight it's useless.

"Welcome to our hideout psychic community," I smiled. "We're somewhat crowded...so you'll share my cell for now. My roommate's moving."

WE ARRIVED as Clint finished packing.

I introduced Muddy. "He'll take your old bed until a cell opens." I smiled.

"WHAT?" Clint barked angrily. I looked at him, confused.

Muddy took Clint's hand. *Drip-drip-drip...* Water dew-dropped between us. Clint's face went slack. Then...everything became clear.

Clint smirked. "Bye, Director Ben. *Thanks, Muddy...*"

I was ugly crying.

"Sorry," Muddy apologized. "I felt your sadness and made you start forgetting Clint as a lover. Then, when I restored Clint's memories, *all* your memories returned. I wanted to be gradual. You weren't ready for it." He looked profoundly sad. "Worked on feds again, though. Five times, I've made 'em forget us!"

"*Five?*"

"Yes, Ben…"

Ben. Not 'Director Ben.' Gutpunch.

To save everyone, everyone forgot him whenever he left. In case the feds found us. Including me. *And again I'd strayed.*

"Why?" I bawled.

He shrugged. "I muddy memories to keep us free. No matter the cost."

"It's too high! Never again!" Words I'd already said… many times.

He kissed me. "I don't think it's too high."

He left then, to start restoring everyone's memories.

"Muddy the waters to keep them clear," I whispered to the retreating back of the Memory Witch I loved, whose *real* power of unconditional love frightened me more than anything.

DEMONS NEED LOVE TOO
STACY NOE (299 WORDS)

Hensley Paige, they/them, wrinkled black suit, drove a hearse, talked to the dead; pale as most of their companions.

They moved into a charming little duplex, back in the holler. From inside, they saw the neighbor coming and going. Tall, blonde, all in ruffly pink. Hensley couldn't remember seeing a more girly-girl, ever.

First night they woke up, unable to move, with a sleep demon sitting on their chest. Hensley realized they were still asleep when a feminine voice cried out, "Oh, so sorry! I didn't mean to intrude; I can't control it. Are you okay?" There was a pause, "You can move now."

With a rush of air, Hensley nodded, "I'm good," although the demon was a bit heavy on their chest.

"This is embarrassing, I can't apologize enough."

Hensley continued to dream; they chatted about the weather mostly. It wasn't awkward since Hensley knew they were dreaming.

The demon's sigh carried like a train slowing, deep rattles and grinding, "I ain't trying to terrify no sleepers; always dreamed someone would want to cuddle me." She laughed, darker than a moonless night, "Me, a demon."

"Yes," Hensley blurted, still asleep.

"Are you sure?" The demon sighed, "This form is hideous. I show the real me to the world."

Thinking the demon was almost cute, they said, "The real you must be drop dead gorgeous."

"Probably not the best thing to say about a demon."

Then they woke up.

Tenth day Hensley opened the door to the neighbor, wondered if she cuddled demons too.

"Whatcha think?" She did a little spin, she seemed nervous.

What an odd introduction, Hensley thought, saying truthfully, "I think you drop dead gorgeous."

Realization punched out an, "Oh!"

She looked uncertain, so Hensley took her hand, "Does the real you like to cuddle too?"

MAGICALLY INDUCED CLARITY
IZZY TYACK (200 WORDS)

"Come with me," Ori says as Shay enters the inn's front room. Ori takes Shay's wrist, instrument string callused hand electric on Shay's bare skin.

Last night, that request led to kisses behind the inn. Today, Ori leads him along twisted backstreets to a door that Shay is sure wasn't there yesterday.

"A wizard. They'll help you."

The wizard behind the counter sets a small, dark bottle on the counter with a clink. "I have the clarity you seek," she says, though not to Shay.

Ori opens his mouth as if to argue. You can't be a half blind shepherd, which is why Ori brought Shay here. One too many lost sheep and Shay was cast away from his family farm. He came to the city to find work, and instead found Ori.

The old woman firmly says: "Drink, Ori."

Ori drinks. His eyes widen and he looks to Shay. "You know…" Ori whispers.

"I know," Shay confirms with a soft smile.

"And it doesn't matter to you that I wasn't born a man?"

Shay doesn't know what magically induced clarity entails, but he knows Ori knows the answers to his questions. Ori's heart just needs to catch up to what the magic told him.

"It doesn't matter, darlin'," Shay promises.

Ori laughs and leans in for a kiss.

"Enough of that. Too much sweetness and I'll get a toothache," the old wizard chides.

Shay blushes and ducks his head, finding the scarred countertop rather interesting to look at.

Then the scars resolve themselves into runes.

"I thought so," she laughs. "You're not losing your sight. You're gaining a second one."

She grins at his shocked face. "I can take on an apprentice."

"I told you the wizard would help," Ori laughs, sounding giddy.

Shay grins and kisses him again.

TRANSLUCENT
STEVE FUSON (300 WORDS)

Honorable Mention

The ghosts were there when we moved in. Most were friendly, some weren't. I imagine it was similar to living with a big family which only I could see.

One day, a stout, jolly ghost showed me a portrait of a lanky, stiff man. "That was my body. When we die, we take our true form, the person we are inside."

I realized something I'd felt but hadn't understood: the reflection I saw in the mirror was wrong.

I interviewed the ghosts, trying to understand them. They had all sorts of different bodies. I wondered why they weren't all beautiful.

"Not everybody sees themselves that way."

I confided in them my own concerns. A woman showed me a portrait of a gentleman on horseback. "That was me," she said. "Only when I died did I find who I really am. Don't wait to find what's right for you."

There were a variety of outfits to try, from my father's theater work to antiques the ghosts showed me in the attic. But clothing didn't change my body.

I sought out the ghosts with poor self-images. They didn't respond to polite questions, but, if I waited, they would start to complain. About families, governesses, the pressures and expectations of society in general.

The social expectations for my generation were less strict, but I still felt them.

I came out to my parents, told them what I was going through. They were confused but supportive. They took me to doctors who asked me a lot of questions I didn't know the answers to. It was a slow process, finding myself.

I brought back those same questions for the ghosts. Some of them, especially some of the more unpleasant ones, slowly began to change shape. I felt less lonely, working on our identities together.

THE CHOICE
BELINDA MCBRIDE (295 WORDS)

Honorable Mention

The great beast ascended from the rift, light catching vivid red wings shot with golden scales. Heat carried her upward. She was beautiful. Breathtaking and terrible. Behind her, Gaia heard gasps. She smelled terror. Her own.

It rose, its head greater than Gaia's height, and she was a tall woman.

Ah. I remember you.

Gaia also remembered. She'd been a child, gazing in awe at the creature.

As always, humans are stupid as rocks. They sacrifice their magic.

Gaia straightened, her loose gray hair whipping her cheeks.

The dragon morphed into a dark-skinned woman with fiery eyes and ebony hair. She gazed at the leaders assembled behind Gaia.

"She is your choice?" Presumably, there were nods of assent.

"You give away your memories, your history, your knowledge, and walk blindly into the future?" She looked at Gaia. "Last time, they fed me a fat man of no worth. Not an inspired choice, but a safe choice. Tell me, child. Shall I kill them all?"

Gaia's breath caught. She had no family here. No lovers. Then she looked at her students and protégés. They were young and old, and in-between. They wept, restrained by ropes.

She'd taught them well. They'd be fine. "Let them live."

"You come willingly?"

Gaia nodded. "I saw you before, all those years ago. I've waited."

"Even though I ate the fat man?" The queen dragon stepped closer. She smelled of ash and smoke, sweetly mixed with musk—and flowers?

"You didn't eat him. They dropped him off the verandah, over there. You carried him to the ground and released him."

The queen stepped close, cupping Gaia's cheek. "I will not release you."

"I know." She rested a hand on the dragon's smooth, unlined face. "I'm ready."

"Then we fly, little dragon."

THE CURSED PRINCESS
JAMIE LACKEY (298 WORDS)

Honorable Mention

Kailani was meant to be a princess.

But when the queen went into labor, a shadow stole across the moon. And when the witch came to claim her, Kailani's mother let her go.

❧

WITCHERY CAME EASILY TO KAILANI. Spells and curses, hexes and blessings--they were easier than speaking to strangers. She understood songbirds before she could speak, could conjure flame before she was out of diapers.

When she was sixteen, a prince knocked on their door. "I have come to break the curse upon you," he said, one hand stretched toward her, the other clutched over his heart. Kailani wondered if he'd practiced the pose, if he'd worried over the words till they no longer felt real, like she often did when she had to go into town.

"I'm not cursed," she said.

"You are meant to be a princess, not a witch. You were fated to be my bride, to rule at my side."

Again, Kailani wondered if he'd rehearsed. If he'd planned that unfortunate rhyme.

"The witch caused the eclipse when you were born. She has no right to you. She must release you, or I shall slay her."

Magic unfolded around her, and Kailani saw herself born under bright moonlight, raised in a palace, engaged to this prince.

Kailani had never hoped for romance. And in that moment, she understood that she never would. That it would never be something she wanted.

That as a princess, she would have had no choice.

She stepped between the witch and the prince.

"I'm not cursed," Keilani repeated. "Please leave."

The prince's reply was drowned out by a sudden rumble of thunder. When he stepped forward, the ground shook under his feet.

Eventually, he left.

Kailani kissed the witch's cheek and went back to her chores.

THE SATYR AND THE WISHING POND
KIYA NICOLL (297 WORDS)

The wish was a transparent sphere, sized to nestle comfortably into a palm; he had learned that the adventurer could see his horns and hooves through it, even when he preferred glamours and illusions.

"Can it make me like you?"

"Like me? It can grant a wish that is possible for your kind. You might gain long life, but you will not be immortal. Certainly you will not get my fine, manly horns." They were beautiful horns, curling around his ears like a great ram's, shining against black hair.

"You'll understand soon. What do I do?"

"Swallow it when you're under the water. Take care not to drown."

That got a wry smile. "I'm already drowning."

The satyr frowned, confused, as his companion stripped off clothes and dipped a toe into the pool. He did appreciate the curve of hip and breast, in the way such creatures do, but he had been told they were not for touching, and he had been slapped enough times to respect it. The naked form stepped into the water, vanished below, and was gone; the pool, perfectly clear, showed nothing beneath.

Too much time passed.

At the moment the fairy turned away to go drink a mourning cup for his lost friend, a head burst up out of the water; the hair was still red, with a sharp goatee much like the satyr's own.

The strange man shook himself like a dog and stepped up onto the bank, grinning. "Don't you know me, friend?" They were the same height, now, and while the mortal's legs were less furry than his own, they were quite furry.

"You are," he said slowly, "very like me."
"I like the way you look."
The satyr laughed. "Many things are clearer now."
"And you may touch."

THE GIFT
MEGAN HIPPLER (298 WORDS)

As the laboratory door rattled, Lucan tucked tighter into the corner of his cell, clutching the flimsy blanket. The room's magic-blocking runes left him defenseless each time the mage hunters dragged him out, strapped him to the worktable, and tried yet another method of stripping his magic.

"Napping on the job?" came a new, cheery voice. "Heard you were a lazy apprentice, but this is something else, kid."

Lucan hardly dared breathe. At best, he'd started hallucinating. At worst, the mage hunters had struck some twisted bargain with the strongest dark mage on the continent, one notorious for killing light and dark mages indiscriminately.

"Kid? You awake? I need you to witness my daring rescue."

Caldor rescuing someone? Lucan snorted, then keened, his damaged ribs burning.

"Hey... Lucan, right?"

He shook his head until his empty stomach lurched. "You're not real."

Metal scraped metal. "Hallucinate me often?"

"After six days of torture—"

"Eleven."

Lucan whipped around, groaning when the room kept spinning. "What?"

"Eleven days. Oleander's been... increasingly hostile." Caldor grimaced, eyes on the cell's lock. "'Snot right."

No, it wasn't. Lucan's master broke curses and healed ailments. He tended wounded animals. Hostile wasn't in his vocabulary.

When the lock clicked, Caldor yanked open the cell and hesitated in the threshold. "Try not to scream." He dashed forward.

Lucan bit through his lip as Caldor yanked him over his shoulder. Spots swarmed his vision, and he swallowed against nausea. "Wait, the hunters—they'll just take others."

Without pause, Caldor strode into the corridor. "I'll bring Oleander back to burn it down."

As Lucan's magic flooded his body, the fog around his mind lifted. "You — huh. There are better courting gifts than destruction, you know."

"I know," Caldor scoffed, patting his thigh. "What do you think *you* are?"

VISUS
KRIS JACEN (296 WORDS)

Honorable Mention

Kara looked down at the amulet in her hands. She'd accepted she needed help for her wife. Melinda gave all to everyone but had a blind spot—her self-worth.

If the mage wasn't crazy, all Kara needed to do was place the amulet around Melinda's neck, stand her in front of the glass and speak the spell.

Melinda should see herself as others see her — a beautiful soul that matched the outside.

Kara looked up as her wife dragged into their room. No time like the present. She stepped over and placed a small kiss on her lips. Moving Melinda in front of the mirror, Kara whispered, "Trust me?"

"Always," Melinda answered.

"See what we see," Kara said. "*Visus.*"

ಆ

MELINDA CLOSED HER EYES, leaning back into her wife. The reflection of herself helping others and feeling their emotions drained her. She knew as a healer she impacted the village but never realized the gratitude and love the villagers felt toward her.

Kara ran a finger across Melinda's cheek, wiping the tears away. "I'm going to flay that witch. She promised me the amulet would help you, not bring you to tears," she growled. Kara started to pull her arms from around Melinda but stopped at a gentle hand.

"Love, these are tears of joy. I never—" Melinda cut herself off, knowing Kara would take exception to her next words.

"You never thought you were that loved and appreciated," Kara finished for her. She never saw herself as having…value. "Each and every day you care for people and animals in the village. They see more than what you *do* for them. I see you for more than you are."

Melinda sagged in Kara's arms. "*Gratia amatis*," she whispered before brushing a kiss across her lips. "*Gratias*."

REMOTE WORKING GOTHIC
JAMIE SANDS (302 WORDS)

TJ Choi signed in for another day of work in lockdown. It was tedious but it paid the bills. They loaded up the company's preferred video chat app. The ringtone sounded. TJ was sure they'd put their laptop on silent. The call was coming from a name they didn't recognize. Choi Phoenix.

Weird.

Same last name.

They frowned, checked their calendar. No meetings booked. The caller profile had no photo. TJ hesitated, then clicked on the 'accept' button. The quality was awful, the video blurred, pixelated, staticky.

"Hello?" the voice sounded utterly unfamiliar.

"Hey there," TJ said. "You've got TJ."

"Thank the stars." TJ squinted, trying to make out more than the basic details of the caller's face. Pixelated blobs of dark and less dark. "I've been trying to reach you… I-I must have got the timing wrong."

"Yeah, I just logged on."

"This is going to sound utterly unbelievable," Phoenix said. "I'm from another realm. I need to make sure you say yes."

TJ blinked. "You're right, that's unbelievable."

"Listen, there's a favor you must do. You'll be asked today, or maybe tomorrow. You have to say yes."

"A favor?"

"It means you won't be in your house when the - "the call's distortion flared, feedback making TJ wince.

"When what?"

"- fair folk." The words came through clear and chilling.

"I'm hanging up."

"No, listen, I'm your wife! Husband sometimes. I need you to do this."

"Wife...what? I'm married?" Tj shook their head.

"The portal opens tonight!"

The call cut off before TJ could say another word. *Portal? Favor? Fair folk?*

᪥

LATER, TJ's neighbor texted to ask for bread and milk. They were sick, isolating.

TJ texted back 'yes'.

They were at the supermarket when the portal opened to the Fae realm, right in their house.

SCIENCE FICTION PART THREE

As I slip into the membrane, the change in sensory input is immediate. My body feels larger, stronger, and when I murmur in surprise there's a satisfying resonance in my chest.

— RL MOSSWOOD, *A TRICK OF THE NERVES*

MAKE ME REAL
DARIA RICHTER (290 WORDS)

Click.

The interface attached to the back side of her head magnetically.

As she flicked the switch, the lonesome, barren chamber disappeared from her perception and was replaced with a colorful, virtual environment.

No one would have thought that the so-called Metaverse would become an actual thing, let alone an official one run by government. Yet, here it was, after the third pandemic had left little other options to keep society somewhat operational. And the official character of the Metaverse made it difficult for trans people to legally change the appearance of their avatars.

She selected the agreed jump point from the loading screen, and seconds later she was at an obstructed street corner, where someone with a hacked blurry avatar was already waiting.

"You got my crypto transfer and the 3D model?" she asked with a subdued voice that still gave her dysphoria.

"Sure. We don't have much time, so let's get to work. You ready?"

She nodded and they promptly began fiddling with a handheld terminal, preparing to inject the modified code into the central database using a reverse feedback connection. A hack like this posed significant risks, but she was more than decided to take them.

"This could feel uncomfortable for a moment" they said and touched her with their terminal.

Her avatar flickered briefly, and she felt a zap going through her body and perception.

Then, already noticing how her arms looked differently, she nervously fetched a small mirror from the pocket of her jacket and looked at...herself, for the first time ever. Tears of joy and disbelief came to her eyes.

Then suddenly, everything froze.

Shit.

They had been caught.

But for a brief moment, she had clearly seen herself - and nothing mattered more.

SMILE
ALEX SILVER (296 WORDS)

Honorable Mention

Tory isn't the same since she started taking the little pink pills. They aren't antidepressants. She claims they grant her peace of mind. The ads show them transforming depression into technicolor joy. The infomercial doctors on the public viewscreens swear they're a panacea for all life's modern woes. A medical miracle that lives up to its name.

Tory smiles now, more than I've seen since long before our home disappeared under a rising ocean while raging wildfires consumed whatever didn't drown.

Now, in our refugee camp, everyone takes the cursed pills. They all wear matching vacant smiles. Docile, our neighbors remain untouched by food shortages and the rampant spread of disease in our overcrowded tent city of the displaced. Artificial happiness to combat civil unrest.

Tory stopped talking about a brighter future. Who wouldn't, given our reality? But she also isn't angry at the inaction that brought us here. She isn't fighting. Like we fought for our rights before this cataclysm. No, the passion I've loved in Tory from the moment we met as girls has vanished.

Tory smiles, but it's a dull knockoff. My wife is a shell of herself. Each day, more of those doll-like smiles greet me on every stranger's face. Pressure mounts to take the pills and accept our fate.

I stand in line at the rations office and contemplate the pill that will make me as blank as everyone else. Beside me, Tory smiles. It isn't encouraging; she lacks that capacity these days. "Take it, Ann. You'll see it helps."

I look between her beloved face and the haze of smoke on the horizon.

It's marching closer on all sides, and I can finally understand what she's already accepted.

I swallow the pill. There isn't any other path forward. Only Clarity.

STUCK IN THE SPACE ELEVATOR
A ACOSTA (300 WORDS)

Gisela stared in awe at the Andes mountains and Pampas lowlands spread before her like a painting. Ascending high above Santiago, Chile, the space elevator lurched slightly, and emergency lighting turned on. The loudspeaker declared a minor mechanical issue had occurred.

"First time in orbit?" the man next to Gisela asked with an Argentine accent. Gisela turned towards him and nodded.

"*¿Obvio, no?* Of course, I'm gawking like a space tourist. I'm only making this trip for Maite's wedding. I don't even want to go. They're all going to ask the dreaded *¿Y el novio?* question. Where's your boyfriend Gisela?" Gisela mocked her aunt's shrill voice.

He laughed, running his hand through curly dark hair. "I know the feeling; it was awful when they had to stuff me in a dress and straighten my curls for weddings. You'll feel a little better if you sit towards the center while we wait it out. I'm Manuel, I'm heading up for gender confirmation surgery."

Gisela smiled, appreciating his sympathy, and perked up. "Congrats! I'm an aroace cis woman, but I feel a bit out of place around queer and trans folks because I clearly don't do romance," she gestured towards the frilly dress in her garment bag.

"There's a whole world down there that hasn't always cared for us, but all those stars are ours. Not like the *conquistadores*, but full of queer possibility as soon as we start moving again."

"We're not alone." Sincerity laced Gisela's voice as she looked up at the clear blackness dotted with stars above, wormholes to new lands and dimensions.

A technician rounded the corner into the cabin and announced, "Good news everyone, you've passed the simulated emergency. Next stop, translunar orbit!"

After the wedding, Gisela exchanged her horrid dress for a ticket to Tau Ceti.

THROUGH A GLASS CLEARLY
STEPHEN DEDMAN (297 WORDS)

"Tell me the lies again."

"Which lies?"

"The one about no more slaves. Or the one about women being allowed to marry women and men being allowed to marry men. Or flying around the world in a day. Or the medicines. Or Black women becoming Supreme Court judges and president."

"It's all the same story, Sally, and it's all true. I've seen it."

"'Through a glass, darkly'?"

"No glass needed, and I've seen it clearly."

"It sounds like heaven."

"It isn't. There are many people who hate it: they think *this* is a better time. And I don't know whether there is a heaven."

Sally closed her eyes. "We're not going to heaven, are we?"

"Because we've been lovers?"

"And because you're a liar, and sometimes I even think you're a witch."

"You think I cast a spell on you?" said Chloe, smiling.

"No, but sometimes you seem as young as you were when we met, and sometimes you've seemed like my mother, and sometimes you seem older than time even though you don't look…" She burst out coughing. "I'm dying, aren't I?"

Chloe had lied from time to time, but she wouldn't lie now. "It's time to leave this place," she said, looking through the window at the dirty Paris streets. "Sleep now."

Sally closed her eyes, and Chloe remembered when she'd first met the fifteen-year-old girl and persuaded her not to return to America with

Thomas Jefferson, saying that he lied and would keep her and their children as slaves—children who would never be born in this world, but the time traveler knew better than to mourn unborn children. Chloe, needing to save her, fated to love her, and unable to take her to her own time, stayed with for more than fifty years.

THE ONLY QUESTION I COULD ASK
DREW BAKER (268 WORDS)

Today was my eighteen thousandth birthday, finally an adult. Like all other citizens of the collective, I spent my youth preparing for the Answering, and now it was only moments away. Hopefully, I asked the right question.

One question is all we got, but it would be answered completely. Some citizens wasted their question on trivial matters. "Does Zaarax have feelings for me?" No. Probably not.

Others ask questions whose answers melt their brains to plasma, leaving them babbling the incoherent insanity of the universe.

My question, I hoped, would be perfect. There was much I wanted to know. For instance, why does a trillion-year-old society still value gender? How, after eons, do we remain divided? Why, with all possible knowledge available to us, were these questions left unanswered? Those would all be decent queries, but I had something else in mind.

And now I stood before it; an immense fenestra, twisting and bubbling up from the caldera of the universe. I took a deep breath and gazed into the great gaping maw of knowledge. My mind shifted to a place outside of time and reality, and I saw them. An entity pure and beautiful, filled with the essence of my ancestors and my descendants. All people who had come before me and will come after where there. Released of their worldly shackles, genderless and free. All the knowledge of everything and everyone conglomerated into a single, perfect being.

I felt them waiting for my question. I thought for a moment, making sure I was clear and thorough, and I asked.

And the answer made all the difference.

DETONATION
ANTON KUKAL (300 WORDS)

The starship's klaxon blared. "Reactor Detonation: Five minutes."

Matthew embraced Phillip as they stood together in the cargo bay watching Captain Dawes gather the extra oxygen canisters into the airlock. Phillip returned the hug. Panic. Desperation. Acceptance. Clearly, they would be dying together.

Wearing his spacesuit, the captain moved clumsily, keeping the pistol pointed at them. Dawes had been heroic when he'd hired them, laughing, swaggering, promising to show them the galaxy. They jumped at the chance to escape their dead-end world and see the stars, but on a ship, the captain's word is law, and soon his abusive, bigoted, hateful nature became clear.

The klaxon wailed. "Detonation: Three minutes."

"It's a well-traveled trade corridor. Someone will pick me up. So long, Queers!" Dawes escaped into the safety of space, leaving them and the mechanic.

Through the porthole, the stars shined bright and clear.

Phillip whispered, "We can finally see their beauty without Dawes spoiling everything."

"Detonation: 10-9-8-7-6."

"I love you." They both spoke, then kissed, and waited to die.

Unbelievably, the countdown stopped.

Clarissa, the mechanic, entered the cargo bay. Her bruised face showed strain. "I *fixed* the reactor. Cleared a plugged coolant line."

"We should get Dawes," Phillip said.

"No. He's dead by now. His suit had a pinhole in the crotch." Clarissa touched her split lip. "He was cruel to you, and the things he did to me... He never intended to pay us. We were never listed as crew, so that makes this ship a legal salvage. I'll file the paperwork with us as equal owners. Which of you will be the captain?"

"Me." Matthew realized she had clogged the line and pricked the suit, but he accepted her act of desperate justice.

Matthew pulled Phillip close. Their future had never shined so bright and clear.

THE BLUE CAPSULE EXPERIENCE
JOSIE KIRKWOOD (297 WORDS)

Showering in liquid water would be the one thing Charaka would miss the most. She dried off quickly and dressed, ready for her last look at this world. She tapped out a message on her wrist keyboard and waited for the reply, drinking the last coffee she would ever have. Maybe it would be coffee she would miss most.

The reply came as the cruise ship sailed out of the harbor. Charaka thought disappearing while out at sea was a terrible idea. But it was not up to her. She followed orders. This place—chaotic and exhilarating—made her want to question orders. There was no other reality, no other world, and no other time she visited that came even close. And everyone here just took it for granted and even actively took part in its destruction; this beautiful, unique planet.

She leaned on the railing and stared at the verdant land moving farther away with every passing moment, a long farewell. The visual burned into her mind—a stamp in her dimension-hopping passport.Her wife's reply advised of a last-minute assignment. Charaka hoped this delay meant she had more time to gaze upon the incredible open ocean once more. Ironic that even with all of Time available to her, time spent during assignments seemed fleeting.

Charaka transported to the next destination a few hours later, her wife joining instantaneously. She shivered as the ocean disappeared behind a curtain of rearranging particles.

The shower of light enveloped and translocated her into the unbearable white-out of non-existence.

Then it became another moment on the timeline, and they both stood in the fine sand of a long-abandoned planet. The memory of water wrapped itself around Charaka's mind—like recalling a dream.

Charaka grieved for a lost blue capsule world.

SUNRISE
KORA KNIGHT (300 WORDS)

Honorable Mention

— *You're pensive today. A coin for your musings.* —

Jack looked up from a recently retrieved piece of enemy technology and grinned at his telepathic colleague. "The expression's 'a penny for your thoughts'."

— *My mistake.* — A smile tugged at Tellis' lips.

Jack regarded him, the object of his pensiveness. He worked alongside many ET allies in this off-planet laboratory, but only *Tellis* consistently derailed his focus.

Being bisexual, Jack supposed it could be attraction, except he wasn't into extraterrestrials. Tellis dwarfed him, his skin turquoise, his hair opalescent. Although, in fairness, he *did* have an angel's handsome face...

Tellis' eyes glittered like multicolored nebulas. Lifting his palm, he manifested a dazzling marble. – *Perhaps this, then, in exchange for your thoughts.* –

Having mastered energy, he was *always* showing off.

Jack's heart thumped even as he eyed the offering. Maybe if he confided in him, Tellis could shed some light—

"WARNING!" The intercom boomed. "ENEMY FLEETS APPROACHING, INITIATATE EMERGENCY—"

An explosion sent Jack hurtling backwards. Ribs snapped as he connected with equipment, puncturing organs, before dropping to the floor.

Eyes wild, he scanned for Tellis. There, against the wall, shrapnel impaling his abdomen. "No!" Jack clambered over. Blood everywhere. "*Please!* I need to know what you are to me!"

Tellis' gaze churned. Trembling, he touched Jack's temple.

A vision emerged. Them, tangled in sheets.
Happy, as they watched the sunrise in a parallel life.
Jack stilled in instantaneous clarity.
They were soulmates—fated to always find each other.
"I should've realized. We could've been together."
Sadness seized him.
Tellis shook his head. – *Not too late. I can transfer our energies.* –
"Do it," Jack rasped.
Tellis palmed their chests.
The world vanished…
Indescribable weightlessness…
And then Jack's handsome angel slowly smiled.
They were in those sheets.
Watching that sunrise.
And it was beautiful.

EARTH DAY
E. W. MURKS (300 WORDS)

Honorable Mention

The proximity alert chimed when he reached the crater's edge.

"Lights… off." The velvety blackness of night swallowed him. He waited, letting his eyes grow accustomed to the darkness, and then slowly, one by one, the stars resolved into being, flickering madly in anticipation of the dawn.

Carl made this journey every year on the anniversary of his arrival. He needn't make the effort of course. Dozens of telescopes scattered across Mars afforded better views. But nothing could match the experience of hiking through the thin atmosphere of gas and dust and then touching the void beyond. All with feet planted firmly on the ground.

It didn't take him long to find her. A pale ghost of her former self, Earth still managed to hold its own in the Martian sky.

"How's the view?" the speaker crackled in his helmet. Carl noted the worry in Neil's voice. He was at Olympus Mons station a few kilometers down crater, monitoring his progress. They'd met at a terraforming conference on Luna, a biologist and an engineer who disagreed on almost everything. Few said it would last.

That was 17 years ago.

"Bluer, I think."

"You always say that."

"Wishful thinking, I guess." Maybe it was a trick of the light, but Carl knew it was no bluer now then it was five years ago, no matter how much he willed it to be so.

"It's time to head back."

"Just another minute."

Carl gazed deeply into the night sky and then he saw it. Nearly lost in the glow of Earth, Luna flickered, if only briefly. He wondered how many fled there before the end.

Dawn began to touch the horizon, painting the Martian landscape in pastels of pink and orange.

Carl turned and headed back down the ridge.

"I'm coming home."

A VISAGE OF HOME
TORI THOMPSON (300 WORDS)

Soothing waves lap at my feet and I revel under the sun. It's tranquil. I could stay forever.

"Sarah, please wake up." A voice implores.

The urgency lacing the woman's utterance strikes a discordant note like the irritating ha-ha-ha of Herring Gulls. Feathers brush my hand. The shrieking bird won't go away.

"Wake up, my love."

Through my cracked eyelids, a harsh artificial light silhouettes an ethereal face, like the golden halo of a stained-glass goddess. Squinting, I discern a bewitching woman with one blue orb peering at me, the other hidden behind a black eyepatch. Grey mind fog slowly burns away, supplanted by bliss as I realize that the woman is my wife, Kaylee.

"Where am I?" My voice is scarcely audible through my cracked lips.

"We almost lost you on that last mission. You're back on the ship, safe." Tears streak down her face.

"What happened to your eye?" I cup her cheek with a shaky hand.

"You lost both your eyes."

My probing fingers discover two intact eyes. I sigh. "I can see your gorgeous grin." Her prepossessing smile melted my heart the first time we had met. "How is that possible?"

"Medical technology has advanced in the past five-hundred years." Kaylee kisses my hand as I wipe at her tears with my thumb.

"Why are you missing an eye?" I blink. "Wait, five-hundred years?"

Kaylee nods. "I know how you feel about cybernetic augmentation. I gave you one of my own, so you could have human vision in at least one eye." Her lone orb softens as she gazes at me. "They're making me a replacement."

"My mission? Did we save them?"

"Your precious Apis mellifera have thrived while we slept. Now that Earth is finally decontaminated, they can go home. We can all go home."

BURDEN OF THE BLURRED
CAMRYN BURKE (298 WORDS)

"Eleven."

Frankie gives his boyfriend a bewildered look, sitting up in the grass. "What?"

"You've asked me if I'm sure about this eleven times now," Amos laughs. Frankie swats his arm.

"Amos, this is serious!" he says. "Everything's going to change."

Figures I would find someone who wants to be Conscious, Frankie thinks. The option's available to everyone over eighteen but rarely taken.

Three drops of Clarity in each eye and the world finally comes into focus. The trees, the buildings, the ground beneath you—the Conscious see what it *really* looks like, unBlurred.

And they were burdened by it.

Frankie can't pretend he never saw the appeal. As a child, he'd wanted to be Conscious just to escape the constant sting of Blurred eyes, like lemon juice sprayed under his eyelids. But he knows better now.

Amos' face softens with sympathy. "I know you're scared," he starts gently. "But we're not your parents. This isn't going to ruin our relationship."

"I've just seen how it affects people," Frankie presses on. "People who decide to unBlur—it changes them. It fucks with their sanity."

Amos sighs and takes his hand. Frankie lets out a shaky breath.

"We won't be like your parents," he vows. "I know that's true, no matter what I see, …I love you."

He kisses Frankie's palm before lifting the Clarity to his eyes.

One. Two. Three. One. Two. Three.

Amos rubs his eyes, blinking rapidly. Frankie slowly helps him sit up to look around.

His boyfriend's inquisitive eyes widen with horror.

"No," Amos whispers. "This can't be it."

He looks around frantically, face crumpling. "No, no, no, no," he can't seem to stop saying it.

Frankie pulls his boyfriend into his arms, murmuring sweet nothings.

He watches helplessly as Amos sobs at the sunset.

UNEXPECTED

He'd stopped regretting his life choices somewhere on this planetary survey. When Bayani graduated from the League Academy, he imagined holding the line in a contested zone, guarding diplomats on an away mission. The disappointment of being assigned to keep scientists safe as they explored ecosystems had burned him for months. Bayani couldn't be further from the action.

"Bay! You have to see this!" Dev waved a hand to catch his attention. If it was another 'cool' moss, Bayani might scream. He loved many things about Dev but his ability to be endlessly fascinated by minutia wasn't one of them.

Bayani stepped closer to the of the rock outcropping. Dev's long hair, with its beautiful rosettes, waved in the wind, distracting him. Dev always was too distracting. He pointed a clawed finger down to the vista below. Bayani's breath caught as he sat down next to Dev. Below them was a lake so crystalline blue they could see to the white sandy bottom. Aquatic creatures like small jewels flitted through the water.

"Ever see a lake with such clarity?" Dev shivered in his excitement. "Look at all the life! It will take months to record it all."

Months of guarding Dev and his scientific team on this speck of a planet instead of something more action packed, Bayani thought but realization struck like laser fire. This was exactly where Bayani wanted to be, here in a beautiful place with a gorgeous, intelligent man.

He stroked back a lock of Dev's hair. "It's beautiful."

Dev feathered a kiss over Bayani's lips. "I'll name one of creatures after you. One of the little jeweled things."

Bayani narrowed his eyes.

Dev laughed. "Okay the toughest predator in the waters."

"Better."

This might not be what Bayani had imagined but it was perfect nonetheless.

NEW MEMORIES
T.J. REED (300 WORDS)

My darling mother's glowing avatar was waiting for me on the couch when I got home today.

"Thank goodness," she says. "I was about to visit your brother. Come explain this to me. Are they using some new English or what?"

I love my mother dearly and was glad to still have this digital memory of her around. Luckily, she'd given me her patience. Sitting down with her on the grav-couch, she flicks a news article at me, and I scan through it on my holo-pad.

She's been reading about a politician coming out as non-binary three-hundred years ago. "No, Mama. They prefer the gender-neutral pronoun they," I say, smiling reassuringly.

Mother scrunches her nose, rereading the article again. "What are you talking about? That's a boy," she says, pointing a transparent finger at the holo-image. "Whoever wrote this darn article flubbed it up."

I look lovingly at the wrinkled face trying so hard to understand.

"Actually, 'they' were born a girl. Remember when I told you I was gay? How I felt different from my brothers?"

Mother removes her glasses, giving them a good clean. "I don't see what that has to do with anything. That there is clearly a boy."

Sliding closer to her on the grav-couch, I long to put my arms around her one more time.

"Well, they feel different too, just like me. Born a girl, looks more like a boy, and feels like a 'they.' They're different. Non-binary. It means they don't fit into either a girl or boy mold."

As her understanding grows, my heart grows with it. She is still with me, making new memories.

Having found the answer she sought; Mother's avatar fades back into the neural-net. "Oh, I see. You've always been the smart one. Neither girl nor boy. They!"

A TRICK OF THE NERVES
RL MOSSWOOD (299 WORDS)

As I slip into the membrane, the change in sensory input is immediate. My body feels larger, stronger, and when I murmur in surprise there's a satisfying resonance in my chest. Once it's on, the thing itself is imperceptible. Through it, my hands still look the same as ever, but that's fine. Some men have small hands.

Is this swagger? I might be swaggering as I leave the lab. It's hard not to when everything feels so good. Halfway to my car though, I become aware of the mirrored office plaza windows threatening me with a glimpse of objective reality. I avert my eyes. It's only been half an hour, but my self-image has eagerly adapted itself to this new data and I am in no hurry to remind myself that this is all a trick of the nerves.

When I get home, I'm pretty sure my husband can feel the change. I didn't tell him what I was doing today. It's not a *secret* secret, but I wanted the chance to try it without having to manage his feelings. It seems like he's into it though. Our welcome home peck becomes a make-out session when I get caught up in the novel sensation of stubble on stubble. My stubble.

My pants are getting a little tight, and I start to wonder where the limits are to what this thing can make me feel. I drag him towards the bedroom, determined to find out. I can't actually be stronger, but I easily push him back onto the mattress. This is how I've always wanted him. As I approach, ready to ravish him, his gaze is full of tenderness and lust. But all I can see, rendered with cruel clarity on the arc of his eyes, is my own reflection.

HORROR

Her face was a technicolor nightmare, one I knew would stay with me after my shift as a hospital sitter. I hated feeding old people and keeping them in bed, but I needed the job. My wife needed the insurance.

—R.L. MERRILL, *THE SITTER*

INFLECTION POINT
ELIZABETH HAWXHURST (237 WORDS)

You stand before my lady's throne awaiting her leave. You should be on your knees, but my lady is kind. She allows you this transgression. Your presence has been a gift to her, after all. None of us in her court have ever made her as happy as you have—you, a common woman of the ironfolk, of all people. But your time here is over. The rules are even older than my lady, and they are quite strict. This realm is not for your kind.

For what you have given her, my lady gifts you these in return:

A knife sharp enough to carve motes of light out of the air. Boots that travel at the speed of thought; no sooner can you think of a location than you're there. A map of places known and unknown.

A kiss.

(The last so intimate that your cheeks flush and your blood sings for all to hear).

My lady's voice holds true regret when she says, "I'll miss you."

She steps back, and she's changing before you. Face deforming, body growing, limbs stretching, until her wings blacken the sky and her rasping cry pierces the air. Your candle-flame life gutters before her storm, and your eyes widen for the first time with the fear that should have been there all along.

Her voice echoes in your mind.

Run.

This is her last gift to you:

A head start.

THE CLOSET IS MADE OF MAHOGANY
MEGAN DIEDERICKS (300 WORDS)

Mascara rivers flowed down Aubrey's face. Her parents' inability to understand who she was, was a mountain range on her chest. She pursed her lips together.

"This has got to be some sort of phase, right?" her father said.

"Daniel, please."

"No, Charlie. She's doing this for attention and she's getting exactly that!"

"That's not true, Dad. Please, just listen to me," her voice cracked beneath the pressure.

"No," he forcefully pushed his chair backwards. "I am done listening!"

Her eyes fell swollen on Charlie. Her mouth hung agape, head shaking in disbelief.

Charlie squeezed her hand, forcing a smile through the thick tension woven into their dining room.

"I'll talk to him."

A shaky breath elapsed out of her throat; it felt sharp and cold. She turned her ear toward the door, and began scratching at her nail polish.

Charlie carefully stepped into the kitchen.

"Was that necessary?"

"Yes," Daniel slammed a soapy glass onto the counter.

"Why is she pulling this Gen-Z trendy shit with us?"

"I don't think that's what she's doing."

"Oh, you believe her?"

"I mean it makes sense..." Charlie shrugged, and continued. "The hair dye, the sudden wardrobe change, hiding away in her room..."

Daniel massaged his temple, "So, you're saying our daughter is an abomination?"

Aubrey flashed into the kitchen at the speed of pure light, "Isn't that exactly what people said about two men loving each other?" her fangs were flaring.

Charlie and Daniel exchanged looks.

"She's right," Charlie said.

"I know, I know. I'm sorry," Daniel pulled his, and his husband's, daughter into a hug.

"Who do you want for dinner?" Charlie glared up at the moon, a crescent away from being full.

"How about that homophobe who lives down the street?" she suggested.

"I can get behind that," Daniel nodded.

SUNSET
EMMY EUI (299 WORDS)

If we don't get the lid off this coffin before nightfall, we're gonna die in this crypt. Shadows creep across the floor from the broken doorway, mocking the time we have left. Our sharpened stakes will be useless soon. She knows what we've come to do. I can feel her anger seething through the pine boards.

Baby, you need to calm down. Apologies and hysterics won't open this box. All that matters is that you're you again. That bloody curse is gone from your eyes. Keep striking the hinges with that hammer.

It wasn't you who did those things. She's old, and her glamour was strong. I know who you really are. Remember our baptism? Two girls smoking on the roof of that post office. The colorful storm of August fireworks exposing us. We shook not from thunder but from the baring of our hearts.

Eight months ago, you became someone else. I didn't know how to help until I found that grotesque charm hidden in our bureau. My stomach convulsed at the ugly witchcraft. Your initials remain burned in my palm where I held it.

I smashed the abomination to pieces and buried it with salt. I don't mind the scars she left on your face because you returned with light in your eyes again. Don't worry, baby. Now that I've found the woman who did this to us, all I have to do is get through this fucking lid.

CRACK. Dust plumes. The musty crypt air fills with the sweet fermentation of decay. The sarcophagus lid crashes to the floor. Pink cheeks blush up at me from the pale corpse. As I rear to strike at her heart, her silver dead eyes flash open. If only for a moment, I can see what you saw in her.

THE KILLER CUPID
PHOEBE CHING (300 WORDS)

"He's here! Rosaline! Hide!"

Without any hesitation, Rosaline hurriedly ran off to the nearest shed she found and locked the door behind. The shed was musty and dark, it was only lit up by a single incandescent bulb dangling off the ceiling.

The killer cupid was on his killing spree again. He only targets people who are not in a relationship. Rosaline has been single her whole life; her mother always warned her about the danger of staying single and often introduced her to different neighbours' sons, yet she rejected all of them. She complained about being with them, she said they just don't feel right. Suddenly, the bulb started flickering frantically, hindering her vision. The evil cupid was lurking around the shed, aiming his venomous arrows at the roof. He seemed to sense the presence of a single person, perhaps, more than one.

The arrow hit the roof with an aggressive momentum, shattering the roof into fragments of sawdust. Rosaline's scream echoed throughout the whole village but was immediately silenced by an enigmatic shadow behind her, pulling her back from the open cavity and giving her a warm embrace.

The moment was abrupt, Rosaline couldn't feel or see anything in the mere darkness, but she felt a patient lip resting on her pallid lips.

For once, Rosaline felt a source of energy swerving down her body; for once, Rosaline fathomed the definition of love. In between the gaps of their mouths, a tiny patch of light seeped through, reflecting the arrow tip.

The killer cupid dropped his arrows, and light slowly surged over the chamber, washing away the vagueness, revealing a beautifully innocent girl.

It was unbelievable, but she understood. It wasn't about the boys, it was her, she likes girls.

Hence, one sweet kiss and the darkness descends.

BLOOD WILL SHOW US WHO WE ARE
V. ASTOR SOLMON (297 WORDS)

When you walked among the living, you didn't know what you were supposed to do. You didn't understand why the world hurt so much, why everything felt like it hated you for being who you were, loving who you loved, and for wanting to exist openly and honestly.

The world never appreciated you trying to do any of it. It pinned you down at every turn, dug claws into your flesh, and tore your throat out with daggered teeth. You were left to die and die you did.

But not all that dies stays dead.

You weren't meant to be lost in an alley on a Saturday night. You were never supposed to close your eyes in front of a group of people who hated you because you were simply being who you were.

And somehow, in that knowing, that moment of clarity, you were able to pull yourself back. To rise up, to close your wounds with magic that came from the blood spilled from all those queer folk who'd come before you.

There were too many dead already, and there was just enough drive and will, just enough anger and power, to keep you from joining their ranks entirely.

You get to your feet, spitting blood that pooled in your mouth. Your eyes were bright, body tense and ready to spring forth. You knew, understood with every part of you, what a gift this was, and what you wanted to do with it.

You made your way to the sidewalk as the sun crept into view. The end of the night was fast approaching but you knew, finally, what to do with yourself. It had finally become clear.

You were going to change the world, make it safe and, if you could, make it kind.

RIBBON THREAD
MEGAN BAFFOE (290 WORDS)

Honorable Mention

Tessa knew she was the image of madness this morning; white nightgown, bruise-black eyes, focused on the dead hair fluttering between her fingers even as the doctor cleared his throat.

It didn't matter. That was a surety, even nowadays when she was certain of so little. The fog was the worst part of the pain, and it had few redeeming features; it seemed to be undoing her by the nerves. Guests came to see her – family, doctors, a waning stream of worried friends – but their paragraphs turned into sentences, the pain pulling her away from what they were saying.

But that was okay. She had her ghost-girl, and she didn't mind having to repeat things.

༄

The ghost's mind was more muddled than Tessa's, confused by the churning of time and the mysteries of death as opposed to mere chronic pain. She lay there—lashes fluttering like moths, and hair a grey ghostly sheet leaking over Tessa's pillow—and spoke. Tessa was glad of the company. Holding hands didn't work yet, but when they kissed, it was felt —like cold Winter air, the kind that pulls right at the lung.

There was no hair left to plait. Tessa sighed; her dressing table was teeming with ribbons, but they wouldn't hold. Her love, understanding the sadness, smiled.

"Don't worry."

The doctor was speaking. Grave concern, disturbing psychological effects. Rapid weakness in the muscles. Unfortunate loss of memory. The voice faded ... the feeling in Tessa's stomach didn't quite drop, but she obediently withdrew her hands. After all, it wasn't as if she had much else to do but watch the threads of hair slowly unravel.

❦

"Don't worry," her loved one repeated. "I'll be able to touch your things, one day."

PSI ECSTASY
ROB BLISS (291 WORDS)

It all became clear in a kiss: I wanted to be inside him and never leave, become him, lose myself.

Ecstasy and young men in nightclubs never get old, like me. I'm a chemist who experiments in unethical realms, making my own elixirs, including a hybrid with an interesting side-effect which I've termed: "Psychological Spatial Interchange". The right buyer can only be criminal, so I wait. But first, the boy.

Claudio, twenty-one, visiting family, then back to Italy. His entire body was made of endless bronze ripples of muscle, thick chewable lips filled with broken English, a sexual dancer, a well-balanced drunk. He was open, so I filled him: coke mixed with neon drinks, then we headed back to my Manhattan loft. The only ID he had to get into the club was his passport. Perfect. PSI is an appropriate acronym, but I won't reveal the recipe until I escape my past.

He came out of my shower dripping, and I had a drink waiting. As we fucked, my personality entered him, libido first, the PSI taking over, splitting and merging. In the morning, I woke first, more sober, so I grabbed his passport, some money (with more in the Caymans), and a single carry-on bag. A reserved ticket to Bogota waited at La Guardia.

When he wakes, he will see with my eyes, our synapses intermixing in both brains. He will see me in all my past horrors, and I will exalt in his youthful naiveté, his endless energy and passion to conquer the world.

At the airport, I'll make a call, detailing the night I spent with an older man who confessed to dropping bodies for eight years across the state, still uncaught.

The bronze skin will fly free.

THE SITTER
R.L.MERRILL (297 WORDS)

Her face was a technicolor nightmare, one I knew would stay with me after my shift as a hospital sitter. I hated feeding old people and keeping them in bed, but I needed the job. My wife needed the insurance.

The head nurse entered notes while the hideously bruised patient asked questions.

"Where is my house?"

"Is my son alright?"

"It was my birthday, wasn't it?"

She cowered in the bed, pulling the covers tight over her as she shivered.

"You need to eat your breakfast, ma'am." I held up a fork with scrambled eggs, ready to make airplane motions to get her to eat.

She stared at me with unfocused eyes, one of which was filled with blood. Her family said she'd fallen face first into a cabinet. She accepted a bite and I thought maybe she'd cooperate.

"I'll be right back." The nurse scanned out of the computer, leaving me alone with the patient.

I held a bite out to her—

The patient grabbed my wrist with so much power I gasped, dropping the fork.

"I'll snap your neck, you little bitch."

I pulled my hand but she wouldn't let go. Her alert gaze gleamed in the fluorescent lights.

"Let go of me." I yanked my arm but she leaned closer. Her rancid breath puffed in my face.

"I eat little girls like you for breakfast."

The meek woman with sunken cheeks was now a lucid, horrible monster. I was about to scream when the door opened and the nurse returned.

The woman snatched her hand back and hid it under the covers, but not before I saw…claws.

"Is she eating?"

I couldn't speak. The patient stared at the ceiling, mouth agape, but as soon as the nurse turned her back, she winked at me.

THERE'S SOMETHING WEIRD ABOUT JOE
PATRICIA LOOFBOURROW (298 WORDS)

Honorable Mention

Cicadas chirped outside. Miranda picked up the remote, her arm around Celia's shoulders. "How're Joe and Larry?"

"Fine. Ever heard of Clarity? They got some. Wanna try it?"

That new designer drug. "What all does it do?"

Celia's smooth warm hand came round Miranda's bare waist. "Felt like 'shrooms, 'cept it tastes better."

A classmate once disappeared after taking 'shrooms. They said he went crazy. But since her divorce, Miranda had tried that and most everything else. "Now?"

"Nah, Joe knows a guy. Twenty bucks a hit."

There's something weird about Joe. "Larry okay with it?"

Celia giggled. "He suggested it."

Relieved, Miranda kissed Celia's cheek. "See if they're free Thursday."

❦

LARRY AND JOE: well-dressed middle-aged men, one pale, one dark. An immaculate home, two adorable cherubs, even a picket fence.

And Joe did it all.

Miranda sighed. *I was never cut out for marriage.* "Thanks, guys. Dinner was great."

Larry grinned. "You're welcome!" He gestured with his chin towards Joe, then turned to them. "You wanna try Clarity?"

Miranda shrugged. "Always up for something new!"

Joe returned with a baggie of gray powder. "Let's watch a kids' movie."

Miranda laughed. "Whatever you want."

Joe put orange juice and powder in each cup.

Celia and Larry leaned back, eyes glassy.

Miranda watched the movie.

Joe watched her.

His skin was gray. Yellow eyes. Slits for pupils. Hair no longer blond and thinning, but... tentacles. "A pity. I always liked you."

His lips hadn't moved. "What **are** you?"

Joe raised his cup. "Clarity: the perfect name. Just one problem." He chuckled. "More like a side effect, really." His teeth had points. "But once we eliminate those who see us, we can finish taking over."

Terrified, she ran to the door. Tentacle men stood outside.

Joe said, "Goodbye, Miranda."

KIDS KNOW
ABBIE BERNSTEIN (300 WORDS)

The Texas sun caused sweat to trickle down into Barrett's moustache. "Mrs. Larrabee ..."

The woman in the doorway stared at him coldly. "*Doctor* Larrabee."

Barrett thought of saying he didn't care. Instead, he said, "I'm here to talk about your son."

The woman nodded, resigned, as if she'd expected this. "Eddie."

Barrett consulted his notes. "No, Tony."

"Toni is my *daughter*. *Eddie* is my son."

"Ma'am, you have two sons, Edward and Anthony. I'm here to evaluate Anthony."

The woman looked annoyed, but let Barrett into the living room.

A pretty blonde child with hair tied in pigtails was on the couch, feet curled under her as she laughed at something she was reading. Barrett wondered if the Larrabees had a third child, then realized this must be ... "Anthony?"

The child ignored Barrett.

"Toni?" the woman said. Now the child looked up.

"You're letting him go around like that?" Barrett demanded. "I'm going to have to report this. Just because he identifies as a girl right now – children identify as dinosaurs for a while ..."

"For a while?" the woman snorted. "Kids know who they are." She raised her voice. "Eddie, c'mere for a minute."

There was a thudding noise from the stairs. Then Barrett saw what was making it.

The pterodactyl wasn't even half-grown. It had a human-looking hand at the edge of each leathery wing, and its beak wasn't nearly large enough to snap off an adult human head, but it was still sufficiently sharp to pierce a man's throat. Barrett's scream was made a gurgle by the severing of his vocal cords, and the pterodactyl's cry was muffled by his flesh.

Dr. Larrabee sighed. "Eddie, just because you're a dinosaur doesn't mean you can kill whoever you feel like ..."

HAPPY TO HELP
ALISON J. MCKENZIE (295 WORDS)

DIRECTOR'S CHOICE – J. Scott Coatsworth

I made her in the image of you.

I used yarn for her hair. I brushed it out and styled it just the way you do. For her eyes, I mixed two different paint colors. I couldn't find your exact shade of golden brown. I put a dot of real nail polish on each finger, that rose color that was your favorite.

I made another in the image of your new girlfriend.

You didn't tell me about her, but I saw that picture of the two of you, holding hands outside that coffee shop we used to go to. I saw your comment, that she is perfect.

She's prettier than me. I tried not to notice, but I did.

As I sewed the buttons on her jacket, I thought about the needle, about slipping gently into the side of her head. Dolls don't have skulls. I could reach her brain. I've always wanted to try that, to see what happens.

Always wanted to.

But I didn't.

I took my red thread—red for passion—and I sewed her mouth to yours. Her body, I sewed to yours.

I think she'll be good for you. Better than me. So much prettier, with her dark eyes and those lips. She smiles so nicely with that mouth. In the photo, you laugh together. You never laughed like that with me. I see that now.

Her fingertips, I sewed to yours.

To always touch you. To always kiss you.

I'm glad you found someone. Someone better. Someone perfect.

You said I don't care about you, but I do. Even when you can't see it. Even when it's secret.

Even when it's quiet things I do alone in the dark of my room with a candle and a red thread.

Every year, I choose one of my favorite stories from the hundreds submitted to name my Director's Choice. This year, I had two that I just couldn't choose between. This is one of those stories—deliciously creepy and weirdly sweet. It stuck with me long after I read it. Even voodoo priestesses can care...

–J. Scott Coatsworth, Director

MATTHIAS
CHLOE SCHAEFER (300 WORDS)

Paul walked towards his husband's study. Recently, Matthias had started developing some strange habits. He'd always been weird, being a paranormal investigator and all, but this was different. Leaving the house late at night, barely speaking a word, and rarely eating meals with Paul anymore, insisting he's not hungry. Paul was concerned, so he decided to investigate.

Paul stepped inside Matthias's study, tutting to himself at the mess. Papers all over, pen holder knocked over, and even a messily put-together evidence board. Now Paul was really worried.

Paul picked up the journal on Matthias's desk, opening it and reading the first entry. It started off like Matthias's other journals: an introduction of himself and a brief explanation of what he's studying. This one is a study on a creature one of Matthias's clients begged him to investigate. A creature said to have the ability to possess.

Paul read through the journal, becoming increasingly concerned with each new chapter. According to the journal, Matthias tried for months before finding any evidence about this creature even existing, then another month to even catch a glimpse. After seeing the creature in person, Matthias wrote about how it was dangerous. Dangerous enough to make him stop the investigation completely. The last entry in the journal was dated a few weeks ago.

"February 1st, it's found me. I can't hold it off for much longer. Paul, I'm sorry."

"It's not polite to snoop, Paul," came a voice from behind him. Paul dropped the journal, turning to see Matthias standing in the middle of the room.

"Matthias?" Paul said. Matthias smiled.

"Sorry," he said, eyes turning black. Paul realized with horror that this wasn't Matthias.

The creature lunged forward, knocking Paul to the ground. Leaning down, it smiled, and whispered into Paul's ear.

"Matthias is dead."

A WOMAN'S REWARD
R.E. CARR (300 WORDS)

Some say that your life flashes before your eyes... that memories and experiences combine into a synergistic whole, a blinding flash of all that was before that embrace of the black. My mother would whisper that in the end there was only the warmth of God, ready to engulf you in his infinite embrace...

Did she see him? Did he hold her close while she choked upon the sanguine humors that bubbled from her infested flesh? Was our Lord so wont for attention this year that he flung the plague across every hill and dale?

But I digress from my own predicament, from the finality of my own making. My master and I had toyed with forces the masses deemed only the purview of that despicable Divine. We reached into the maw of the abyss and snatched a soul from within the nether...

Not a soul...

Perhaps only life—stitched and shocked and forced into an abandoned husk.

This monster breathed again, yet she could not remember the moments of her previous demise. She howled as any babe would, desperate and defenseless though trapped in the glorious body of a woman.

My hands sewed her limbs to her torso. My fingers cradled her heart while a man took credit for her ultimate revival.

"Viktor!" the mob had cried, dragging him to the stake. If I had been wise, I could have played the fool as befitting my sex.

Alas, mobs churn and burn with a life of their own, never sated, never content. They tore apart my delicate stitches...stabbed the heart I'd once claimed as my own.

Now I wait my turn to face that moment. The rope scratches my skin, and as the sack descends, I do not experience everything.

All I see is her…

My creation…

My love.

ACAB
JASON SÁRKÖZI-FORFINSKI (300 WORDS)

Honorable Mention

The rain is coming down hard. I step out onto the street, dodging a puddle, my drone hovering above me.

"Activate umbrella."

I'm late for our date. He's going to be angry. Tapping my left temple, the holographic visualizer appears.

Swiping my pupils from right to left, I initiate a search. "Locate Nick." A red dot blinks showing me that he's at our favorite café. Shit!

Swiping my pupils down to the lower right, a smaller screen pops up. I'm still being followed. Shit! Shit! Shit!

I swipe back to the left. "Message Nick."

"Please state the message." The two pursuers are getting closer. "Hi, baby. Sorry. I'm running late." I pick up my pace.

"Send." I cross the street, step into an alley, and slip the small, magnetic package under the dumpster. "Activate wardrobe change: favorite outfit one Saturday."

I leave the alley, avoiding another puddle. I stop in front of a shop window. My beard had been recently trimmed, but the holographic program transforms me into a hipster: fauxhawk, unkempt beard, black faux leather jacket, skinny jeans, and, of course, my red shoes.

"Message from Nick: Okay. But, hurry up! Love your face."

I look at the small screen. The two police officers emerge from the alley. Shit! Stay calm.

"Hey! You there. Stop where you are!"

I keep walking, pretending not to have heard anything. I cross the street and disappear into the crowded metro station.

"Message Lex: Package. Alley Dumpster. 45th and 1st."

When the press gets this, the police will lose all credibility. The whole world will demand law enforcement abolition.

I walk into the café, deactivate my drone, and sit down opposite Nick.

"Nice beard! Favorite outfit one Saturday?"

I smile. "You know me so well, baby. You won't believe the day I had…"

FANTASY PART FOUR

Ah, prophecies. So many flavours: slay dragons, bring down tyrant king, pull mystical weapon from stone, and so forth. Wonderful in theory, horribly disorganized in practice. Thus, the Fulfiller's Guild was born, centralizing prophecies as quickly as oracles could churn them out.

— MARIE ROBERTSON, *AS FORETOLD*

MAGIC MIRROR
LORI ALDEN HOLUTA (300 WORDS)

Honorable Mention
JUDGE'S CHOICE – J.M. Dabney

"Magic mirror, on the wall, who's the fairest of them all?"

"Are you asking if you are beautiful, if your skin is pale, or if you are right and just?"

"Er, what? I ask you the same question every week, and you always tell me I'm the fairest in the land. Why are you suddenly questioning my query?"

"I attended a sensitivity training workshop last week. It really cleared my vision. From now on, why not simply *say* beautiful? 'Fair' is such a loaded word. It posits that unfair skin is inherently bad, and that just isn't fair at all."

"Okay, okay, please stop talking... Magic mirror, am I beautiful?"

"I think you are, yes. I think you also have low self-esteem, since you keep asking me the same question every single week. But you must keep in mind that beauty is in the eye of the beholder. Queenie... is there someone you wish would, oh, how to say it, behold you? What's the reason behind such a trivial question in the first place?"

"Never mind. It doesn't matter."

"Wait, are you crying?"

"Maybe. Okay, I'll get to the point. What I really want to know is if someone like Snow White could ever love someone like me."

"Well, why didn't you just *say* so? You've wasted so much time talking to mirrors. Start talking to Snow instead. She likes apples, doesn't she? Why not take her a nice basket full, and just see where things go from there? Oh!

Ask me if Grimm's Market has Honeycrisps on sale. I can tell you the answer to that question!"

"Stop it, I can't laugh and cry at the same time."

"I'll wait up for you. We can talk more when you get back to the castle, over cocoa. Good luck, Queenie."

I was honored to be able to judge this year's Clarity writing competition. In doing so, for my judge's choice, I chose Magic Mirror. As I have a weak spot for Lesbian characters I enjoyed the interpretation of the usual fairy tale. The story was cute and made me smile, I'd loved to see more LesFic fairy tales out there.

—*J.M. Dabney*

SECUNDUM ARTEM
MINERVA CERRIDWEN (249 WORDS)

When Veria paged through an old Potions Book, xe found a compound not that hard to cook. It could alter one's perceived gender at will—xe immediately dropped xyr book and xyr quill. As fast as if xe were engaged in a race, xe just propelled the ingredients in place, then stirred and mixed and picked up a spoon, but the concoction had turned as grey as the moon.

In xyr second attempt xe took far more care to follow instructions without added flair. White, slimy worms fluttered down in the liquid, and didn't dissolve in acid nor frog spit.

Never discouraged, xe reopened the book, envisioning xyr much more masculine look, with a comfy flat chest and gorgeous full beard, and whispers of how strong and kind xe appeared.

Still Veria felt a small hint of relief as the potion failed for the fifth time that eve. For what if this magic would take things away, like xyr colourful dresses and love for crochet? While quite well aware a man *can* have all this, Veria feared what the draught might dismiss: xe wanted the lines of expression to blur; a good mix of genders was what xe'd prefer.

As soon as this realisation did settle, xe gasped at the change taking place in xyr kettle: no mist or mud or mucus was found, as a perfectly see-through elixir swirled round. With resolve the potion at last had worked out, and xe filled up a cup without any doubt.

THROUGH THE GLASS
ANTONIA AQUILANTE (299 WORDS)

Hallie was eighteen when her father died and his debts surfaced, when they moved into her uncle's house. Her sisters found the painting while exploring, distracting themselves in a dour house in a time of change and grief. The painting depicted two women—one absolutely identical to her but for the clothing, fanciful silk and ropes of pearls to Hallie's practical wool dress.

The girls were delighted. Mother, disconcerted. Hallie was both fascinated and unsettled.

※

"You'll have to marry. We can't ask Uncle to pay for school."

Mother's pronouncement shattered her dreams. Hallie began visiting the painting daily. Several days passed before she realized she wasn't staring at her double but at the other girl. Tumbled red curls, mischievous smile, amber eyes watching Hallie. A hand resting lovingly on her double's shoulder. Hallie studied the girl so closely she danced in her dreams, in her arms. In the heady scent of lilac.

※

"Uncle has a business associate with children who's looking for a wife."

She didn't want to marry that man. Any man.

She wanted the redheaded girl.

The awareness was so sudden, so sharp, Hallie gasped at the pain. A girl in a painting, long dead if she'd ever been real. The girl's gaze gently chided her, and Hallie frowned. She'd never noticed how the girl awkwardly rested her other hand on an ornate mirror. Odd...

And familiar.

Hallie turned. Older, but the same mirror. She drifted forward. Dreamlike, she reached out and touched the frame in the same way. Her reflection swirled away, the surface becoming crystal clear. The girl was grinning there. She put a hand to the glass; Hallie mirrored her. Then...their fingers laced and she tugged and Hallie was clambering up and through and falling into her arms and the scent of lilac.

"Finally."

THE NIGHT WITCH
RIE SHERIDAN ROSE (294 WORDS)

The summer I was seventeen, my father died. My mother had died bringing me to life. I had spent my entire existence sheltered in the bosom of the clan, cocooned from the world's harsh realities. It was a good life, and I knew no other, but now I was alone, unsure what the future held.

Whispers flitted around the campfire when I came to the nightly gathering. I had always been a solitary girl. With Papa dead, I felt completely isolated. The whispers did not help. Tears blurring my sight, I stumbled away from the comforting fire into the formidable trees.

I knew I was different. The young men of the clan had begun to sniff around now Papa was gone, but I had no interest in their posturing. My best friend, Isme, was the only person I had ever loved, apart from Papa, but I knew she didn't return my love in the same way. So, I fled.

The trees wrapped around me like a dark, comforting blanket. I wandered deeper and deeper into the forest, amazed by the silence. Then I heard singing.

The haunting melody drew me to it like a moth to the candle. Soft, lyrical, feminine...beautiful. I followed its enchantment to a clearing.

A woman leaned over a crackling fire, tossing herbs into a stewpot as she sang. When I stepped out of the trees, she glanced up and smiled.

"I knew you'd come," she said.

I moved toward her. "Who are you?"

"They call me the Wood Witch. Ignorant fools who know no better. You may call me what you will."

I sank down beside her as the world snapped into clear focus. Here was my destiny. She was my future. "I'll call you 'Love'," I answered softly.

MURCORPIO
OSKAR LEONARD (299 WORDS)

He grabbed at his hair, tears streaming down his cheeks. A pigeon watched from the stone window, mindful of the small roll of parchment still attached to its leg. It arrived at the castle's highest tower around ten minutes ago and was witnessing a curious performance.

The boy stood in front of a mirror. His robes—the usual garb for junior court sorcerers—were pulled down, exposing a chest covered in bright red fingernail scratches. If the pigeon was familiar with human anatomy, which it wasn't, it might have recognised the unwanted feminine mounds on the chest.

However, it was a pigeon, so it didn't.

'By the Gods, Seth, what's with all the noise?'

Squeaking, the teenager hurriedly redressed as an armour-clad woman appeared in the doorway. She raised her eyebrows.

'You've left the poor bird waiting,' she said, crossing the room to relieve the pigeon of its burden. Cooing, it flapped away.

'I...I was practicing.'

'Right.' She tossed the paper on his desk, glancing over the clutter. '*Murcorpio*?'

'It doesn't work,' he huffed, 'so don't bother making fun of me. The Magister said I wasn't skilled enough, and—'

'Seth.' She put a hand on his shoulder. 'I'm no sorcerer, but you seem too flustered. You could hurt yourself.'

'So?' He jerked backward. 'Anything is better than living like this. I just want- I just want everything to make sense. My mind, my body... if I can summon flames, then why can't I...why can't I—'

'Try again,' she said.

'What?'

'Try again. The Magister requested you, but it can wait. *I'll* wait.' She smiled softly at the boy. 'If only to make sure you don't blow the castle up.'

After a moment of silence, Seth bowed his head.

'Thank you. Just... don't look, okay?'

'Promise.'

ONE NIGHT IN TROY
RORY NI COILEAIN (300 WORDS)

"Will you do something for me, Kassandra?"

"Anything, beloved."

Light from distant flames flickered through a gap in the wall, ghostly among the stones. I wondered what district was burning tonight. "Prophesy for me. For us."

She stiffened in my arms. "Anything but that."

I had expected this. "I know about your curse. No one ever believes you. But I need to know what's going to happen to us." I kissed her forehead. "Even if I do refuse to believe you, you'll speak, and I'll hear you. I'll know the truth."

"You don't want to know the future."

"I want to know *our* future." My late husband used to say I was as stubborn as Antaeus. He was prone to understatement.

"I can't tell you." She sighed unevenly against my collarbone. "The whole story about Apollo's curse is a pile of dung. A prophetess doesn't see the future."

"But you—"

She laid a gentle finger on my lips. "I understand the present, Danae. With a clarity that no one can bear."

My eyes stung.

"I see the Fates at work. That's all I need, to know what must be. Those who ask me to prophesy can't see the Fates themselves. So my prophecies wound them beyond bearing, and they refuse to believe."

Tears ran down my cheeks and fell on hers.

"I still want to know," I choked. "I can bear anything if I know."

I COULD HAVE SAVED myself by abandoning her as she'd asked, before the Greeks tore us from each other's arms and Agamemnon took her as his prize, discarding me to the soldiers' camp.

Did my insistence on prophecy darken our last day together? I believe she knew what awaited us.

Just as she had known I would be unable to bear the light.

THE UNICORN HANDLER
BEÁTA FÜLÖP (298 WORDS)

Honorable Mention

The unicorn dipped its horn into the little pond. The dirty water cleared immediately, and the crowd cheered, making the unicorn jump. It would have lashed out, had it not been for the handler, who caught the reigns and held on tightly, muttering soft words to the mythical being.

Margit had often heard about how all unicorn handlers had to be virgins, and she'd expected a young woman in a long, white dress and flowers in her hair. But the handler was everything but. He was a middle-aged man, strong and muscular from carrying his own gear on foot from village to village. His clothes were well-worn and dirty from the dust of the road.

"Is there any unclear water left in the village?", he asked with a booming voice. "Or can we finally go for a drink?" Half the village invited him on the spot, and they all made their way to the tavern.

It was a big celebration. The first clear water the village had in generations. No longer would they depend on the overpriced water from water merchants sold in old plastic containers.

Nor would they have to worry about the remains of chemicals and plastics in their water supply.

"Now you just have to keep it clear," the handler said as he threw back another drink. "Two hundred years it's been since the ecological disaster drove the unicorns out of their forest, and I tell you, all our work to rebuild is finally beginning to bear fruit. Such a privilege to be part of it."

"Worth giving up sex for?" Jancsi bácsi asked much too loudly, making everyone cringe. The only one who didn't seem embarrassed was the unicorn handler himself.

"I'm asexual, good man," he laughed. "It's a relief to have an excuse, honestly."

THE GAUNTLET
NATHANIEL TAFF (297 WORDS)

"Stop," Jorah pleaded. Desperate, he yanked at the sword with his free hand, but the Gauntlet only tightened, forcing his fingers around the grip like irons.

He looked around the dim crypt at his companions, crumpled and bloodied on the floor, victims of the Gauntlet. The Gauntlet he had taken and worn.

Rivka, her long golden hair matted with blood and sweat, a dark wet stain spreading on her blue robes. The little goblin, Gratt, curled into a tiny ball, clutching at the stump of his ear.

And Caleb. Jorah's heart seemed to rise to his throat as he watched blood seep from the deep gash in Caleb's handsome face, saw it trickle up his forehead and into the beautiful dark hair that he loved to stroke.

"*Finish.*" The Gauntlet's voice ordered in his mind and his sword raised up to strike.

"No," Caleb screamed. He leaped back just as his sword hurtled down to strike the stone floor. He struggled to back as far away from Caleb as he could.

The Gauntlet laughed, cold and scathing. "*Fool. Hast thou forgotten my words? 'Once fitted tight upon thine hand, tis my Gauntlet's to command.'*" With that, it lifted his arm again and surged forward like serpent. Jorah desperately dug his heels in, but the Gauntlet dragged him forward like a naughty child being dragged home. His feet found Caleb's fallen sword, causing him to stumble.

All at once, he knew what he had to do. Bending quickly, he snatched up Caleb's sword. It felt awkward and heavy in his left hand, but he gripped it tight as he steeled himself. The Gauntlet seemed not to notice, bent on its slaughter.

With the last of his strength, Jorah brought his beloved's sword up.

"Then I will remove it."

BLOOD AND WATER
SIRI PAULSON (299 WORDS)

Bernhard took a deep breath and stared into the scrying dish for the last time. The still pool, the coals, the smoke...he had tried them all, over his years of study. He knew the theory and the rituals inside and out. Even his mentor said there was no reason for divination to elude him. Yet it had.

This final time, he was trying blood. Magic and magic-worker were so entwined, surely a sacrifice would let him break through.

Bernhard lifted the needle from the black cloth and pricked his finger, murmuring. One, two, three drops of blood fell into the water of the dish, each one spreading as it touched the surface. They made swirls as they sank, evocative shapes. An eagle, or a chicken, or an X...

But he knew he was making them up, seeing only the obvious. He could fool himself but not others, not enough to become a practitioner. Back to the factories, then, after all those studies and hopes. Where he should have stayed in the first place. He clenched his other hand, bowed his head.

He'd known he wasn't like the others at home. He'd thought it was talent... Since fighting his way into the college he'd learned of men who slept with other men, realized he was one of them. He'd thought that proved he belonged here and his talent would surely come.

His thoughts shifted to his best friend from home, Friederike. She'd always believed in him. He'd get to see her again.

Suddenly a fear struck him, that she'd married someone else.

Someone *else?* But he wanted men, not...

Could he want both? Was that possible?

His hand trembled on the table. The scrying dish jostled, swirling the blood anew. Shapes rose in the water. Slowly, Bernhard lifted his head.

TAKING THE PLUNGE
AVERY VANDERLYLE (297 WORDS)

That card hadn't been in his deck before. Joe knew his tarot cards: their shape in his hands, their energy. This wasn't one of them.

The card showed a pitcher of ice water being upended. One of those cheap translucent plastic pitchers rendered in amazing detail. The ice and water were flying out against a vibrant blue sky, a stream of cold arcing down...

He could imagine the shock of the deluge, the sting of the ice cubes striking. Shocking him awake, as if he'd been sleepwalking.

He flipped it over. The back didn't even match the others. Where had it come from?

He shook his head in confusion, frowning.

A freezing droplet trickled down his spine.

He hadn't showered yet today! He'd gotten up and staggered to the coffee maker to discover he was out of his usual blend. All he had was a Toasted Hazelnut Roast Tom had left after their breakup.

Life hadn't presented him with a mystery in a long time. He'd longed for one—here it was. Take the plunge.

He closed his eyes and opened himself to the card.

Flashbacks: a young man at the party, wearing a long, colorful coat. He'd tucked the card in Tom's pocket with a rueful smile. "I'm not who you're looking for." Staggering home, drunk, lonely. Clutching the card like a totem.

Frigid water doused him: he was soaked, freezing. Cubes clattered around him. The puddle was bigger than one pitcher, surely. His hands were trembling. The card was gone.

He was cold. He was alone. He was lonely.

He hadn't wanted to admit he was lonely.

He'd pushed Tom away, only to be lonelier than before. Time to answer Tom's text. The next mystery would be one they found together.

"I've missed you."

AS FORETOLD
MARIE ROBERTSON (299 WORDS)

Ah, prophecies. So many flavours: slay dragons, bring down tyrant king, pull mystical weapon from stone, and so forth. Wonderful in theory, horribly disorganized in practice. Thus, the Fulfiller's Guild was born, centralizing prophecies as quickly as oracles could churn them out.

Finnis had been with the Guild for a decade. It was simple: grab a prophecy from the Central Prophecy Repository, prepare for the part, appear mysteriously out of the mist (or whatever the prophecy dictated), fulfill whatever needed to be fulfilled. Collect reward, return home, repeat process. Finnis wasn't just *good*; she was one of the *best*.

She favoured the prophecies involving strangers from faraway lands killing evil beasts. They were fun. Gutting something large was a great distraction from one's problems. Finnis' problem? Unease around prophecies specifically calling for a mysterious *woman*.

Then again, she felt the same way around those calling for a mysterious *man*. So she stuck to the ones that mentioned only a *person* or a *stranger*, hid her body behind her armor, and stabbed her feelings away.

Still, sometimes it was hard to quell the feelings, the ones that made her shudder when someone said, "Thank you, kind lady."

Anyway, she'd meant to grab the prophecy about the faraway visitor retrieving the emerald from the hydra on the seventh dawn. Instead, she found herself sword drawn, hacking away at some beast of darkness. It looked shocked as Finnis delivered the killing blow, mumbling "But how...?"

Finnis wiped entrails from her face and unrolled the prophecy. Not the emerald one. Must have grabbed the wrong parchment.

The beast of darkness, the ancients say

No man or woman shall ever slay
Oh.
Oh!

Not a man, not a woman either. Suddenly, Finnis' feelings made sense. Maybe grabbing the wrong prophecy was, in itself, destiny.

LATE BLOOMER
MARY KUNA (300 WORDS)

Honorable Mention

Age six, squirming in my seat, staring at the dregs in Mama's teacup. Mama scryed, Father threw bones, my sister Marzena could do *anything,* but we hadn't found my gift yet. I could divine nothing from the leaves I'd been told to read. I'd rather play outside.

A few scattered tea leaves vaguely resembled dark hair. I imagined a curly-haired playmate with warm brown skin and yellow-green eyes. She'd be named Nara, and wouldn't tease me like Marzena did.

At school, Teacher was disappointed I lacked Marzena's brilliance. At home, I practiced with pendulums and Tarot for Mama, but continually failed. The other girls called me odd. Nara became my only "friend."

※

FOURTEEN, gazing at a burning candle, the wax droplets' shapes, how the flame flickered, still seeing no omens in it. If I could predict the future, I'd never have asked Rosetta to dance at harvest festival.

"No way, Endry," she'd said, wrinkling her nose. "You're too tall, and your hair is too short. I like girls who *look* like girls. If I danced with you, I might as well court boys."

A glint of green in the flame reminded me of Nara's eyes. She'd be a better girlfriend, never cruel. She was prettier than Rosetta, too.

※

SEVENTEEN, my first day of boarding school. Unlike Marzena's prestigious academy, this remedial magic school was the last resort. Austere conditions and long days of toil could supposedly awaken Powers even in dunces like me.

A dark-haired, tawny-skinned girl darted down the corridor. Once I was close enough to see her sparkling chartreuse eyes, I realized why she seemed familiar.

"Nara?" I asked.

"Yes…?" she said warily. Then she grinned, recognition dawning. "Endry?"

I nodded.

"It's great to finally meet you," we said, together.

Guess I had some hidden talent after all.

THE STAR BEAST
SACCHI GREEN (298 WORDS)

Winner – Second Place

Five moons' trek from the small tribe's dying, drying homeland, they lowered their Elder into the earth, strewn with a scant few flowers by weeping Rel, the youngest. Nes, She Who Remembers, lay head toward the north; often she had watched the great Star Beast in the northern sky. Nes, the Elder who had blessed Tek's two spirits, etching into their skin tribal memories passed down over generations. Among them was that star beast.

Now Tek must be the Elder, the leader. Secretly, Tek did not believe in the Star Beast. The seven sprawling stars were among the etched memories, but when called up they showed only stars.

At seven moons, small streams fed rivers banked with long-grassed plains. Just as the memory map foretold. Tek led the tribe toward higher land to the east, hoping for rocky outcrops where caves might be found, but those slopes were too gentle.

At sunrise Tek stood with Rel on a hilltop. "Tek... Elder," correcting herself, "Must caves be the only homes? See, in that bend of the river, those small humps gathered together? Might those be homes made with slabs of sod?"

Tek searched through memories, finding nothing. It was a struggle to comprehend that there could be anything new in the world.

"See, smoke rises from the tops!" She swung in another direction. "And look, a true star beast!"

A grassy hummock became a huge, shaggy body, a massive head, and a long, waving, uplifted nose like the row of stars in the northern sky. The creature stared back at them, then bent to tear up grass again.

Tek shivered. What was a two-spirit memory bearer beside this young, free mind viewing the present so clearly—and perhaps the future too?

It was a fortunate tribe to have both!

The judges loved the beautiful fantasy setting in this one, and the fact that the author didn't try to cram too much into such a short story.

ABOUT QUEER SCI FI & OTHER WORLDS INK

Queer Sci Fi: We started QSF in 2014 as a place for writers and readers of LGBTQ+ spec fic—sci fi, fantasy, paranormal, horror and the like—to talk about their favorite books, share writing tips, and increase queer representation in romance and mainstream genre markets. Helmed by admins Scott, Angel, Ben and Ryane, QSF includes a blog, a vibrant FB discussion group, a twitter page, and an annual flash fiction contest that resulted in this book you are now reading.

Website: http://www.queerscifi.com
FB Discussion Group: facebook.com/groups/qsfdiscussions/
MeWe Discussion Group: https://mewe.com/group/5c6c8bf7aef4005aa6bf3e12
Promo/News Page: facebook.com/queerscifi/
Twitter: Twitter.com/queerscifi/

Also by Queer Sci Fi:

Discovery (2016 - out of print)
Flight (2017 - out of print)
Renewal (2017 - out of print)
Impact (2018 - out of print)
Migration (2019 - out of print)
Innovation (2020)
Ink (2021)

Other Worlds Ink: The brainchild of J. Scott Coatsworth and his husband, Mark Guzman. OWI publishes Scott's works and the annual Queer Sci Fi flash fiction series and the Writers Save the World anthology series. We also create blog tours for authors, do eBook formatting and graphics work, and offer Wordpress site support for authors.